I0761819

PRAISE FOR EXILE OF THE SKY GOD

"Readers should enjoy the constellation of twists that makes this a shimmering heroic romance with a message of hope through transformation. **An effortlessly grand fantasy** that should ensnare young and older fans alike."

— *Kirkus Reviews*

"An odyssey towards atonement is the backbone of P. Anastasia's fresh, lively take on Egyptian mythology, *Exile of the Sky God*. ...**[A]n entertaining portrait of ancient Egypt.**"

— *Foreword Reviews*

"[A] gripping story that is filled with discovery, revised purposes, and new visions of gods and men... **[T]horoughly engrossing and satisfyingly unpredictable: a powerful read, indeed.**"

— *D. Donovan, Senior Reviewer, Midwest Book Review*

Exile of the Sky God

ISBN 978-0-9974485-7-3 Also available in pb, audio, and ebook
Library of Congress Control Number: 2018967234

Other books by P. Anastasia:

Fates Aflame
ISBN 978-0-9974485-3-5

Fates Awoken
ISBN 978-0-9974485-5-9

Dark Diary (Paperback / Special Edition Hardcover)
ISBN 978-0-9862567-8-3 / 978-0-9974485-1-1

Fluorescence: The Complete Tetralogy
ISBN 978-0-9862567-7-6

 Published by Jackal Moon Press

www.JackalMoon.com

Cover layout by Graphix Goddess Design

10 9 8 7 6 5 4 3 2 1

First Edition

Pursue your destiny!

EXILE OF THE *Sky God*

1

MAJESTIC amber and virulent copper feathers draped my body, each crowned with pure ivory fringe. I envisioned sparkling plumage sprouting from my shoulders, spreading toward my wrists like wildfire and igniting my skin with a shimmer of nature's finest auburn tones.

I would have them soon—the most glorious wings, in the vein of my mother, Isis, whose brilliant iridescent feathers glittered like rare gems and whose wings cradled me when I was a babe.

They would be granted to me at my coronation ceremony, where I would also be appointed to the position of Sky God.

Soon. Very soon.

I gazed out at the Egyptian horizon, watching as clouds broke in two, yielding as Amun Ra's aura swept across the land, his all-consuming rays signaling to the world that it was time to begin anew.

The sun god, Amun Ra, reigned supreme over sky, earth, and all the deities in the Palace of the Gods. Lotus blossoms flourished and thrived with his blessings or shriveled and shrank away at his touch. Wheat and papyrus rustled in the wind and swayed in worship when he cast his glow upon them.

Even the mighty Sobek, powerful and fearless god of the River Nile, with his weathered, ferocious crocodile form, lowered his head to the King of the Gods. Ra was the head ruler of all Egypt: the one god whose likeness and name the pharaohs assumed, hoping to attain a fragment of his immortality.

Ra came into being with the face of a falcon but chose to assume the features of a mortal man in order to set himself apart from the animal-faced lesser gods. Although he exhibited no other physical animal features, Ra was anything but a man. His eyes glistened with fire—golden light that mirrored the sun's volatile nature—and he towered above us all, possessing astonishing height, vigor, and poise.

As our king, he appointed and commanded a court of other gods to do his bidding. Some were his brothers and some his sisters, but most were children and grandchildren. All had been molded not in his image, but as anthropomorphic beings with features reflective of their duties.

The warrior goddess and protector, Bastet, had the face of a fierce lioness. She watched over both Ra and the current residing human pharaoh. The powerful, formidable lioness goddess also had a fondness for me, and was like a mother when my own became but a phantom in the light. Bastet kept her feelings secret, as Ra forbade gods to favor one over another. By his decree, any and all allegiances or offspring were to transpire only from cosmic obligation and necessity, and deviants would face severe punishment. As protector of the crown of Egypt, Bastet's loyalties were to rest solely upon that priority—not consorting with me.

Taweret, the hippopotamus-faced goddess of birth and fertility, had a belly eternally round with child, and she carried with her always the joys and burdens of childbirth.

Then there were Isis and Osiris—overseers of mortal life and death—whose faces closely resembled a common man and woman. Isis was the supreme mother of all, caretaker of children, wives, and mothers, but her overwhelming duties robbed my childhood of her presence.

As guardian and ruler of the underworld, Osiris ensured that justice be granted to every soul who deserved it.

Together, they had a single child—me.

Preordained to become God of the Sky, I was forced to don the guise of a falcon's face, even though both my parents appeared human.

As I grew, I observed and studied mortals from afar—the same mortals I would someday oversee—and I struggled with a myriad of audacious thoughts.

Why was I forced to bear the face of a bird, when neither of my revered parents had to do the same?

My mother's wings flaunted the colors of malachite, lapis, garnet, and turquoise, and each feather was trimmed in pure gold.

My golden falcon eyes were mighty and bright, but set upon a backdrop of plain, pale feathers in browns and beiges. Who would worship a god of such... *simple* features?

Today I would become a true god. Ra would surrender guardianship of the sky to me, and my feathers would change. Today marked my coming of age, and it felt *long* past due.

In preparation for my coronation, I shed my avian face and assumed the form of an exotic human—those whom (I had been told) traveled across the ocean from the far Northwest. Though rare, other gods had witnessed foreign voyagers with hair as fair as wheat, and it was my wish to stand out amongst a crowd of beastly gods.

"I am ready," I called to Bastet, who waited for me past the threshold of my chamber. The clinking of bracelets signaled her approach, and I turned to face her.

"You look beautiful today," I said, reaching up to stroke the back of my hand across her fluffy, sand-colored muzzle. Her eyes narrowed joyously and her whiskers could not hide the gentle blush of color flushing her cheeks.

"You are kind, Horus, but you should withhold compliments while in the presence of a god."

I forked my fingers through her beaded headdress. Golden fur from her short mane prickled around her crown and her ears twitched.

"I will be a true god soon, Bastet." I tipped my head defiantly. "Then I will say what I please, and even Ra will not stop me."

"You will never be able to say what you please," she replied firmly. "You must always be wary of your words."

"You will see my power rise with the sun. Once Ra bestows upon me my fated gifts, the wheat and barley will cower before me. The ibex will bow their mighty antlers, and the great ibis shall follow me wherever I go."

Black swelled in Bastet's eyes and she lifted her paws to clasp my forearms. "Please do not speak this way in front of Ra," she said, the pitch of her voice rising. "I have no children of my own, but you are like a son to me. Ra is strict, and he will not tolerate your insolence if you test him."

I shifted my body and forced her paws away, quickly adjusting my bejeweled armlets.

"I will be fine, Bastet. Wait and see." I gestured for her to follow me.

We traveled down a grand limestone hall as we headed for the courtyard—a place of ceremony and gathering—flanked on both sides by enormous paintings featuring animals from the mortal realm below. Though I had seen it hundreds of times, I paused to more closely admire a colorful image depicting an ibis with its massive wings spread wide as it soared over the River Nile. I brushed my fingers across raised strokes of paint and grinned.

"May I remind you," Bastet whispered, "Ra has little patience. We should hurry."

"Yes." I nodded and heaved a sigh.

Several demigods—those with less jurisdiction in the land of mortals and more in the kingdom of gods—waited outside the courtyard. As I passed, they bowed shallowly toward me, which provoked me to sneer. Trapped in the limbo of un-acquired power, but destined to attain it, I was not quite above, nor below them in stature, yet.

After the ceremony, they would bow fully to me, and their foreheads would touch the floor when I passed, or they would pay a grave price for disrespecting a god.

I approached the covered entryway to the outside courtyard and drew the scarlet linen curtains to the side to enter. As I released them behind me, I overheard Bastet apologizing to the demigods for my actions.

She should not have...

The courtyard was vast and laden with thrones arranged in a wide circle around a demanding centerpiece—an enormous cauldron burning with eternal white fire, fueled by the imprisoned kas (lifeforces) of Ra's adversaries.

Gods surrounded me, with Ra having already taken his place in the tallest throne at the center of the circle. My mother, Isis, sat in the throne to his left, and the throne to his right was empty—awaiting his protector, Bastet, who immediately moved past me to claim her seat. My father could not attend because he could not abandon his duties of overseeing the souls of dead mortals; not for a moment.

The crowd let out a gasp as I approached, and Ra's eyes widened with disbelief.

"Why do you wear the face of a man?" Ra spoke, his deep, booming tone resonating through my sandals and into my bones.

Isis smiled and then rose as if to stand to greet me, but Ra swung out an arm to stop her.

"Stay," he ordered, and she swiftly lowered her face and cupped her hands together in her lap, easing back down to her seat.

"Horus," Ra raised his voice again, "I demand to know why you came to your coronation with the features of a mortal man—and a Northerner, no less?"

"You assume the face of a mortal pharaoh, always," I replied, lifting my chin. "So, too, do my mother and father. Why should I not?"

A reddish glow ignited in Ra's eyes and he pushed up off his throne to stand and point a rigid finger my way.

"How dare you question your king!" A ring of colored flame swirled around his hand.

Isis slid from her throne and onto her knees beside him. "Please, my lord," she cried out. "He is only a child and does not understand humility."

"I am no child, Mother." I curled my hands into fists. "I have not been a child for several centuries, despite you and our lord's desire to suppress my powers as if I am one."

Seeing my mother, in her pure, vivid white dress, groveling on her knees before him disgusted me.

Ra glanced at her as she cowered before him, and he shook his head. "Humans cannot fly," he answered, glaring at me.

"My mother has wings, and they are the most exquisite I have ever seen, and yet she presumes the body and face of a human woman. She is no less powerful because of it."

"You are..." Ra began, speaking through gritted teeth. "You *will* be God of the Sky. The humans will expect the face of a regal bird, not a boy."

My jaw tightened at his comment, but I held back my pride. I wanted power, and I would not get it if I continued arguing with my king.

"I will do as he wishes, Mother," I said softly, kneeling beside the cauldron in the center of the room. It angered me to have to relinquish my ideal face, but I had no choice. Bastet was correct to assume Ra would chastise me for it.

I exhaled slowly and allowed my features to transform back into their natural ones—my face growing longer and my nose sharper, swooping down to form a hard, black predator beak. Feathers pierced through my flesh and cloaked the fair golden hair I had become fond of, and my eyes turned dark brown as my pupils enlarged.

"Now stand and return to your throne," Ra demanded of Isis.

She tried to compose herself as she stood and sat again, avoiding eye contact as she folded her brightly-colored wings across her lap.

Ra took a step down from his throne and approached me, raising his hands high above my head. I wanted to look up, but thought wiser, and remained where I was, my eyes to the floor.

"As king," he started, a humming noise sounding above my head, "I decide how magic is distributed."

The marble flooring did not reflect great detail, but with my sharp, falcon sight, I could see that he was conjuring an amulet of power—my birthright—and the stone that would grant me my place amongst the gods. Red light circled the piece, casting a crimson glow around me.

I held my breath as he lowered his hands and brought it closer.

Then a loud crack rang out, and I lifted my face to see my amulet—the entirety of my pre-ordained destiny—sliding across the floor. I scrambled after it and scooped the massive garnet cabochon into my shaking hands. A deep crack had split the stone down the middle, but its gold setting kept the pieces clinging together.

"What have you done!?" I roared at him, cupping the shattered stone between my fingers. "My... powers..." I gasped and struggled to find the words as anger swelled in my chest. "This amulet is my birthright!"

"And it is *my* right to decide when you are worthy of it!" Ra scowled. "If you speak one more word against me in my own court, I will retract the piece altogether." He pointed at me and I pulled the damaged necklace close to my chest.

"No," I muttered, clasping it tightly.

Behind Ra, my mother had her hands over her mouth and her eyes wide with fear. Beside her, Bastet fought to hide her own look of disbelief and horror.

I did not need their pity...

"Ra, please." I looked away and lowered my voice. "Please... my lord. Might you reconsider?"

"You are not ready," he replied with a hiss, and turned away from me. "Let it be known to all, that those seeking independence and individuality within my court will face it alone and powerless. Do not challenge me. I have bestowed upon you *all* your titles, *and* I can strip you of them."

He turned to me and whispered, "We are finished here. Go." Then he said to the crowd, "The ceremony is over."

I heard shuffling as the other gods cleared out of the room, but I could not find the strength to raise my head to watch their disappointed gazes judge me in passing.

All I could do was remain on my knees, clutching the shattered semblance of my true destiny in my hands, unable to subdue my shuddering breaths.

After the room had quieted down, a bright white dress dragged across the floor; my mother approached and bent down to embrace me around my shoulders.

"My dear son, do not be upset with our lord," she said softly, brushing her fingers through my feathers. "He is just and there is goodness in all his actions."

Isis believed that to be true of *everyone.*

I did not.

"How could you let him do this to us, Mother?" I looked up into her brown eyes. "How could you allow him to disgrace me like that?" I could not stop my voice from quaking. "I-I deserved that power!"

"And you will gain it all back, in time," she said, prying the amulet gently from my fingers. "I promise you."

Cold metal against my bare skin made my feathers perk up momentarily as my mother bestowed upon me my amulet, adjusting the gold beads near my shoulders and shifting the cabochon so it was centered below the base of my neck.

"What am I to do with this useless thing?" I touched the stone and grimaced as my fingers grazed the fissure in the center.

Her hands rested on my shoulders in a way they had not since I had been very small. "Prove yourself to him and he will make this right."

I wanted to take my human form again, to show her that I could be strong even in the wake of defeat, but I was too weak.

"I am sorry, Mother." I reached up to wrap my arms around her and bury my face against her long, ebony hair.

"You will always be forgiven, Horus. Come now." She stood and tugged at me to make me stand. "You must rest and prepare for your new duties tomorrow."

I staggered to my feet and looked around the empty room. Even Bastet had been forced to leave me in order to save face in front of our king. I would not blame her, though. She had always been my strongest ally and closest friend, despite her assigned loyalty to Ra.

"You are right, Mother," I said, taking in a deep breath and rolling my shoulders back. "I will prove myself to him, at any cost."

2

SHATTERED and scorned from the embarrassing display at my coronation ceremony, I returned to my room and lay down on my bed, willing the ceiling to vanish so that I could gaze upon the pale blue sea overhead. My face changed again into the human form I preferred, and I rested my hands behind my head and stared up at the open sky.

I had come of age, and my powers *should* have been bestowed upon me properly. Yes, I had taken the face of a man for the event, but with Ra doing the same, I should not have been punished for it.

I lifted the garnet cabochon into my fingers and brushed my thumb across the surface. The amulet was lightweight and the stone as cold as ice, an indication that it contained only a meager amount of magic.

Centuries I had waited for the now useless thing that dangled at my neck.

Tears welled in my eyes; I released the amulet and brought my hands to my face. Childhood ended long ago, but weaknesses associated with it lingered within me, and I could not resist the urge to weep like a child—a child with no mother to comfort him, because she had dedicated all her attention to the mortal children of the world instead.

My face grew warm, my breaths hastened, and I rolled onto my side to face away from the sky, as it seemed to mock my tears with its bright, cheerful display of color. I willed it away.

The ceiling rematerialized and the room darkened, now lit by only a few distant candles eternally burning in sconces along the walls.

Moments later, there was a soft rapping at the archway to my room—the delicate tapping of bristly fur. Bastet. She had likely heard my distress as her enhanced, huntress hearing allowed her to pick up on the most subtle of sounds.

"May I enter?" she whispered.

"You should not concern yourself with me," I muttered, swiping moisture from my cheeks.

"That is for me to decide," she continued, and passed the threshold of my room.

I remained with my back facing her. "You should be guarding Ra, not consoling the failure of the sky."

"A great god such as Ra does not require protection always." She sat on the edge of my bed and her weight sunk in beside me. "Do not be ashamed of your gift, Horus." Her tufted paw stroked my shoulder as tenderly as her airy voice filled the air. "You are powerful, still."

I rolled onto my back and looked up at her. A shimmer of candlelight bounced off the pristine lapis stone hanging from a gold chain around her neck and I grimaced, diverting my gaze as tears threatened to pour again.

"What am I with this scrap of broken magic Ra has given me?" I sat up and crossed my arms.

"You are a true god," she added with a smile of encouragement.

"I am the shell of a god." I reached up, grasped onto the shattered garnet, and tore the disgraceful thing from my neck. I reeled back my arm and tossed the necklace away.

"No!" Bastet swiftly caught it by the chain with her deft, lioness tail. She brought it to her lap and cupped it between her paws. "You must not damage it further."

I narrowed my eyes at her. "So you admit that my strength is broken?"

"Not broken," she replied without raising her voice, "but bound." Her mossy green eyes glistened with assuredness as she smiled. "The boundaries of your magic are restrained only by the walls which you have erected on your own. It is not only the stone which grants you your power." She clasped the amulet tightly and whispered an incantation I had not heard before. A halo of fiery crimson light surrounded her paws, then dimmed and faded away.

"Please take it back," she said, revealing a no longer fractured stone. She had masked the fissure somehow. "Do not allow the appearance of weakness to dampen your potential. Ra cannot suppress your magic, despite his attempt to do so."

I had heard stories about gods' powers rising and falling like the tides, based only upon the faith of the mortals below, but I did not believe those stories.

Our eyes met and I cupped my hands around her paws. "Do you think I can do this? Do you believe the people will accept me?"

"Yes." She nodded confidently; the faith in her eyes convinced me she spoke only truth. I released her paws and lowered my head. "Wear it proudly," she added, placing the necklace around my neck. "You are no less a god than any of us."

Her paw rested upon my shoulder and I looked her in the eye.

"Now that you are a god, you should visit your people," she said.

I gasped. In my rage over the broken amulet, I had forgotten the rights of passage that accompanied it. Before one's coronation ceremony, it is forbidden to visit the land of mortals; now that I had been given the sacred piece, and my status had been made official, I was free to roam the land below.

"Can I? Can I go now?" I asked, standing. My heart raced and a grin drew across my face. Excitement bloomed in me as I imagined myself amongst the humans. There was so much to learn about their ways, and very little that I could acquire by continuing to watch from afar.

Bastet stood and tipped her head, her long, beaded locks of fur clinking together melodically.

"Show them your power, Horus, and you will see how their prayers strengthen you."

"Yes, Bastet." A renewed sense of strength filled me and I felt myself standing taller and straighter. I filled my lungs with a deep breath and exhaled. "I will prove myself to them and to Ra."

"That is the proud and determined Horus that I know,"

Bastet said. “Learn about your people and gain their faith, but do not allow them to know you. We must protect and observe only.”

I scoffed and shook my head. “Why would a god wish for anything more than that?”

“These are the rules we must all abide by.”

“I understand. Now I must go.” I lifted my hands and wriggled my fingers eagerly, watching sparkles of silver dance between them—magic born of a god. I closed my eyes, concentrated, and within moments, a brilliant flash of light consumed me and I vanished from my room.

A howl of joy erupted from my mouth as I shot across the desert sky in a blaze of lightning and thunder. Clouds parted and sunlight washed over my skin as the wind combed through my hair. I soared over a field of wheat and watched it bow. I imagined myself as a mighty eagle, riding the currents with wings as wide as a crocodile is long.

The banks of the River Nile came into view, and I brought my arms in close to my body and pivoted, diving straight toward the water. I penetrated the surface like a spear and then curved, twisted quickly, and burst back out toward the sky.

Animals could not see me, and neither could nearby fishermen, but they all pulled back in surprise as a splash of waves sprouted up out of the still water. Birds scattered from the reeds at the wayside and took flight. Grand, crane-like ibises, with black faces and pearly white wings, joined me as I flew, as if they were drawn to my presence.

Their inherent obedience reiterated the fact that I was destined to be prince of the sky and reminded me that I sought an even greater fate than that.

"Look there!" I shouted, pointing at the riveting golden light overhead. The birds did not turn, but I carried on. "Someday, I will choose when dawn and dusk occur. I will vanquish the serpent Apep, whom Ra battles each morning for custody of the sun, and I will cloak the earth in light as I please. I will control when you awaken from your nests, when farmers plant their crops, and when you should fear winter. The sky is only the beginning... The humans will see me for my true potential."

I flapped my arms and willed an extraordinary pair of wings to take shape, the feathers reminiscent of my mother's. They were illusions, but the manifestation planted a seed in my heart that sprouted into courage.

I soared across the land and focused on the massive city up ahead. If I could not earn the respect of Ra, then I would earn the faith of the people of Egypt.

3

I SELECTED a calm spot in the crowded marketplace and landed silently in the shadows behind a tapestry vendor's wooden stall. People scuttled to and fro, some stopping to look over the vendor's wares, and others passing by without taking notice.

A flick of my hand sent a gust of wind zipping toward the overhang, tugging various wall hangings up and making them dance and twist in the air before they went tumbling back down against the stall table.

The shop owner, whose name I had overheard was Aket, scrambled to keep his merchandise tidy and organized, straightening each tapestry and flattening out subtle wrinkles caused by my trickery.

Placed off to the side was a pile of smaller hangings bound together by rope. A familiar face decorated one of them—a falcon-headed god which was not Ra, at least not as I knew him. Clearly an artistic rendering, the likeness was loose and far from accurate. But it *was* a falcon-headed god, nonetheless, and I did not appreciate the shopkeeper hiding such a face from his customers.

With a stroke of my hand, I made changes to the tapestry so that it would reflect my own features. Next, I unbound the thing and let it fly freely into the air, causing a commotion amidst the crowd as it darted and dashed like a kite with no lead. It rose toward the sun and cast a shadow over the shopkeeper's stall, attracting a frenzy of people who crowded around to watch. The attention made me laugh, and I finally decided to pull the tapestry from the sky and back down into frazzled Aket's hands.

With word of a "magical tapestry" buzzing through the streets, Aket was quickly swamped with overzealous buyers. Between sales, he scooped up the wall hanging I had enchanted and spirited it away to the back of the stall, where he raised it high and nailed it to a thick wooden beam.

"I am keeping you," he said, smiling upon my image. "You are a special one, and I thank you for the profits and good fortune you have brought to me this day." He lowered his head and briefly closed his eyes. "I am your humble servant."

My hands tingled and I turned them over. Ripples of energy forked through my veins, binding with my spirit and strengthening me from the inside out. The small burst of magic filled me with confidence and reassured me that I could, in fact, enhance my abilities by earning the faith of those in the mortal realm.

The prospect prompted me to start thinking about who else I could try to impact and what types of humans might be impressionable and easily swayed.

With some instantly coming to mind, I willed myself to

be transported to another place.

In a flash, I stood in the center of a room surrounded by a circle of sitting children—all boys of varying ages.

I glanced down at the floor. My pristine golden sandals had become dingy and worn and shabby linens clothed my body. I lifted my hands and observed the deep wrinkles creasing my weathered palms. Then the arms moved against my will and the clothing shifted, a whoosh of lifeforce propelling through me as the school teacher took a step to the side, his body no longer assimilated with my own.

The teacher stretched out an arm and gestured to some symbols on a wall, demonstrating the stroke order and shape of each with a piece of charcoal. Next, he pointed toward the sand and instructed the children to reproduce those symbols.

As the little boys began scratching words into the sand by their feet, I bent and watched, noticing how their dark eyes glimmered with fearlessness, creativity, and hope. Their pulses quickened as they hastily worked out the words, each boy trying furiously to finish first. Upon completion, they raised their gazes toward their instructor and held their breaths. I sensed excitement and eagerness in their minds; it was nearly time for class to end.

One little boy had not completed the assignment yet, and he struggled to decide which stroke would come next, his hand trembling, his fingers uneasily grasping the twig he used to practice. He was the smallest of all the children, probably no more than four or five years old. His clothing was far more worn and tattered than anyone else's in the room, and a tinge of adoration for this little one bloomed in my heart.

His marsh-green eyes narrowed with intense thought and his lips wrinkled with frustration as he would ready himself to draw the next line, but then pause and shake his head, as if he was unsure and afraid of making the wrong choice.

The instructor walked over to his side, crouched down, and then guided the boy's hand in the correct path to make the characters forming the word 'mother.'

With the work complete, the instructor stood and dismissed the children from class. All the boys rushed out of the building to head back to their homes. All except the little one who had struggled with his writing.

"Fenuku!" his teacher addressed him, standing by the entryway and waving for the child to come. A small rope and carved wooden animal toy dangled in his grasp. "Come now. It is time for you to return home. I have your little hound."

The small child continued to sit, cross-legged on the sand, tracing the character over and over again. Fenuku, his name meaning 'one who was born late,' turned toward his teacher and gasped. One look at the jackal toy and he sprang up as quick as a rabbit, dropped his writing instrument, and then hustled toward the teacher. Fenuku's foot hit the ground at just the right angle that his balance shifted and he went tumbling forward. His knee smacked against the steps of the entryway and he let out a yelp.

I watched as the teacher eased the boy up into a sitting position and turned him around so he could take a closer look at the injury.

An unusual feeling squeezed at my insides and an

uncomfortable sensation caused my lips to pull downward as Fenuku revealed a bloody gash across his knee. Tears welling in his dark eyes must have been the byproduct of the human sensation 'pain' other gods had spoken of. Physical pain was not something I had ever experienced.

Judging by the child's sad face—the redness flushing his skin and the water pouring from his eyes—I did not need nor wish to experience such a terrible thing.

The instructor retrieved a cloth from a pocket in his robe and used it to pat the boy's wound, dabbing bright red blood away with gentleness not unlike a devoted mother. Fenuku pulled his knee in close to his chest and rocked back and forth.

I approached them both and lowered a hand to the child's crown, concentrating until a faint glow came to the tips of my fingers and a spark of golden fire swept across his forehead. It faded into his skin and then a gush of wind whisked through the room, causing a spiral of sand to dance across the floor. The boy gasped and released his hands from his knee.

"What is it?" the teacher asked.

"My knee. No more pain," he replied, slowly peeling away the cloth to reveal fresh, new skin at the site of the wound. "It is gone."

"It cannot be gone, Fenuku," the teacher countered, squinting and glancing over the knee several times. "It was bleeding only a moment ago." He took the soiled cloth into his hands and turned it over so the blood faced out. "It bled."

"It really is gone!" Fenuku leapt to his feet and skipped about in a tight circle.

"But... how?"

"Mother says gods were with her when I was born, and that I am strong," he said, smiling. "The gods have healed me."

The look on the teacher's face was one of disagreement and skepticism, but he nodded and acknowledged the boy's words with a grin. "Yes. You are strong." He handed Fenuku his wooden toy jackal and walked him to the entrance. "I will see you tomorrow." He waved goodbye and the child hurried home.

"The work of a god?" the teacher said to himself, now that the boy was out of earshot. "I am not sure I believe that. Children heal quickly. Perhaps..." He glanced down at the crumpled, bloodied cloth in his hand.

I sneered at his disbelief and flicked my hand, sending the fabric from his grasp and out the archway, into the streets, and then away into the sky.

The teacher stood with his mouth agape.

Another spark of magic prickled my skin and I experienced a minute spike of strength. A whirl of accomplishment and pride swelled in my chest.

I had done it again. A tiny miracle had caused a new glimmer of energy to manifest inside me. If these petty acts were all it would take to become a grand god, I would surpass Ra in no time. With greater magic, greater feats could be possible.

In time, whole villages would acknowledge *and* worship me...

The remainder of the afternoon was spent filing through neighboring streets and marketplaces, watching how people interacted and moved about their day.

Then the sun faded below the horizon and the goddess, Nut, raised her hands and released her star children into the sky.

By now, I had wandered into the depths of the city, to a place illuminated with oil lanterns that cast swaying, ghostly figures against the sand. The people there looked different. They were rough in appearance, with unkempt facial hair, muscular features, and loud voices that echoed through the stone alleyways, almost as if they had wanted others to hear them. They carried dingy blades at their sides and took lumbering steps.

They spoke of treachery, infidelity, and theft—words I did not comprehend. So I followed the men into the night, listening intently as they discussed profits and revenge. Unsure of their intentions and with my curiosity piqued, I tailed the small group down into a darkened cavern near the edge of town.

I moved along with them until the animalistic sounds of a man in distress caused me to pause and wait behind the group. They could not hear nor see me, but even as I clung to them like a shadow, the feelings evoked by their company were disconcerting. I wanted to leave, but I would not allow my cowardice to stunt my knowledge.

The source of the grunting and straining noises became visible, and I drew nearer to watch. The man was older than those in the group I had followed, his hair peppered with the color of limestone, and he had deep-set wrinkles creasing his forehead and the corners of his mouth. He was likely a grandfather, at his age, but why he was bound in tattered ropes and rusty old chains, I was not certain.

Foul words were exchanged, and moments later, a younger man revealed a corroded, primitive handsaw. I stood stunned, watching, even though every inch of me wanted to flee. I was too captivated by the horror which was the saw-bearing man relieving the old man of his hands by separating them at the wrists.

"The gods cannot save you now," the man wielding the blade growled, then he cursed his victim again.

Blood pooled on the floor; the old man's death was imminent.

Could I heal him? Could I heal such a violent wound?

I could try...

Shock had pierced me, replacing energy with weakness and making me feel hollow inside.

A plume of sand flitted through the air, kicked by the assailant, and then the old man fell to the ground.

Fear consumed me.

I squeezed my eyes closed and willed for it all to go away.

All of it!

Be gone!

Soothing heat and warm light enveloped me.

I opened my eyes and found myself in a familiar place. Tall sandstone columns and delicate paintings of nature and earth surrounded me. The sensation of discomfort had left me, but an unfamiliar heaviness sunk in my stomach.

I took a deep breath and sighed. The palace was quiet and calm. Predictable.

Humans were volatile and strange, and I had yet to learn what it was that made them act the ways they did. Gods are rigid and stable, and do not stray from their intended duties. At least, that was what I had been raised to believe.

After Ra shattered my amulet and crippled my powers, I had begun to believe otherwise.

I had not come so far only to allow the destiny of the Sky God to slip through my fingers. I would recover my courage and face the human world again tomorrow.

4

NUT GRACEFULLY swept her arms around her twinkling brood of stars, gathering them from the sky in order to make way for Ra's arrival. As he rode his gleaming chariot across the desert horizon, I readied myself to face the morning of a new world.

Bastet had come to visit again, and approached me meekly, her furry paws clasped together, and a small but encouraging smile curling her feline mouth. "How was your first day amongst the mortals?" she asked, her eyes glistening with hope, and her fuzzy, rounded ears facing forward attentively.

I did not wish to tell her the truth about what I had seen—a violent act, which had ended with a man's soul being propelled to Anubis for judgment.

"Appalling," I replied with a groan, vividly recalling the pool of bright crimson spilling toward my feet after the incident.

"Why do you say that?" she asked, reaching a paw toward my cheek. Bastet had a way of sensing inner turmoil. It was part of her gift as a warrior and protector to evaluate the intentions of others swiftly and with great accuracy. "What did you see down there, dear Horus?" Her paw pad stroked my cheek tenderly.

I crossed my arms and tried to force the horrible sight from my memory, to no avail.

"Tell me, please." She spoke in a motherly tone that could coax a secret from a corpse.

"I witnessed the brutal death of a man at the hand of another," I replied.

"I see," she uttered, her paw slipping from my cheek down to my shoulder. She inhaled deeply. "Mankind can be cold and violent toward one another. As goddess of war and protection, this is something I have witnessed before. But even I cannot defend them all. We strive to promote justice and peace, but the mortals do not always strive for the same. Even the gods cannot inhibit the free will of man. I am sorry you had to witness a terrible act, but I assure you, there is good in the mortal realm. It is our responsibility to discover and cultivate it."

She smiled wide, her ivory fangs glimmering in the light. "I saw what you did in the marketplace. It was entertaining to watch humans scurry about after those tapestries. And that child, I am sure he has renewed faith since you healed his wound."

"Do you believe so?" I gazed fondly into her crisp, leafy-green eyes.

"You are capable of great things. Continue learning, gain the faith of others, and your powers will increase until you are strong enough to bend the clouds to your will. Visit the temples—they are the foundations of our magic."

I had heard about the temples of the gods, places where subservient mortals gathered to pray and request assistance. There were many, each devoted to a different deity, but I did not believe there was yet one devoted to me.

As if she could read my thoughts, Bastet said with encouragement, “Faith and magic are abundant in *all* temples, Horus.”

“Very well,” I replied with a nod. “I will visit the mortal realm once more. I trust your words, and I am grateful for your faith in me.”

The journey back down to the city was not quite as exhilarating as it had been the day before; the heavy, moist air and ominous grey skies sapped my energy. Still, the brisk morning current against my skin reminded me of my newfound freedom.

Ibises waddled along the banks of the Nile, and nearby crocodiles became hesitant to strike their prey, as if out of respect for my presence. A herd of ibex galloped over the rocky cliffs on the far side of the river, and I caught sight of two males smashing their knobby antlers together like battering rams. They were fighting over mates, though I doubted the visually intense fight would end in the death of either party.

In the distance, tall obelisks—temple markers clearly defined by colorful paintings—towered above other structures, identifying places of worship. Surrounding priests and priestesses dressed unlike other villagers, their clothing consisting of light, white linen with decorative accents and collars embroidered with golden and scarlet threads. They were not dressed for heavy work, such as farming or masonry, which was evident by their clean, well-kept sandals.

I entered the first temple I came upon, which was dedicated to my mother, Isis. In the center of the room was a large, but shallow, pool with lotus flowers floating on the surface. The sacred water was clear and clean. Lit candles of various heights surrounded me, and the temple walls had been lined with colorful motifs painted by a skilled hand. A tall, detailed statue of Isis stood at the head of the pool, carved from the finest basalt and polished to a grand sheen. I approached her and gazed up toward her face; it did not resemble my mother, to say the least, but it was a fair enough resemblance that I recognized the vain attempt. The statue was much taller and larger than the real-life small, frail goddess who was dwarfed even more by her grand, magnificent wings.

The statue's wings appeared to be attached to the arms by bracelets, and its hands rested on the lap, making the wings drape down the thighs of the seated figure. Gold accents had been added to her headdress and jewelry, but the rest of the piece was charcoal in color.

One feature that did mirror the true Isis was the eyes. They were dull and without emotion, seeming to stare off into the depths of nothingness, as if she was preoccupied. It was her sworn duty to assist and protect mothers and children, but the Oath of the Gods strongly discouraged feelings from being shared between one another. Even from a mother to a son...

Isis was loving and kind to mortals in need and to mothers who called upon her for help, but she turned a blind eye to her small falcon-headed child crying in the shadows of his lonely room.

By law, it was her duty to leave me devoid of her affections, but I had eternally wished otherwise.

Memories of a turbulent childhood rattled me, and I shook them off quickly, escaping the temple so that I might forget my woes elsewhere.

There were so many gods in Egypt that temples nearly outnumbered homes. Many of us were worshipped, some more ardently than others.

The next temple I came upon was to Bastet, my dearest feline friend. Her place of worship was far smaller than Isis', and the walls inside had been lined with shelves, upon which people had placed mummified pet cats. While Bastet had never sanctioned the murder of her race, those that had died of natural causes were a welcome sacrifice in return for protection and guidance. Cats were sacred and beloved by many. They kept mice and rats from the storehouses, protecting the farmers' vital food supplies. Having one in the house could also dispel evil spirits and curses, so mortals worshipped them nearly as much as they did us.

I bowed my head, paying my respect at Bastet's temple, and then left to find something more suited to my needs.

With an abundance of attendees, a temple of Ra might be the opportune place to find willing disciples. Although I suspected Ra would not be appreciative of his followers' faiths being swayed, he was too busy with his own duties to notice a few stray sheep.

Deeper in the city, I came upon the monstrous building which was the Temple of Ra. Twice the size of the one erected for Isis, it stood several stories high. The entrance had been paved with the finest granite stepping stones and both sides were flanked by tall, majestic pillars that towered above me. Each had been decorated with illustrations of Ra in various poses: hunting, fighting, commanding an army, and sitting upon his throne in the sky. Hieroglyphs detailed his adventures, fleshing out the facts in poetic, ostentatious fashion, making it clear the author had taken creative liberties with his dramatic retellings of Ra's battle for the kingdom in the sky.

I passed several columns as I neared the main entrance and gazed up at the golden sun inlaid in the cornerstone overhead. It had been artfully set facing the East, so that the sun might shine upon it and cause a remarkable glimmer in the early morning.

Limestone statues depicting pharaohs—physical representations of Ra—sat one at each side of the archway. They were sculpted with large, defined muscles and stiff, masculine poses, and their watchful stone gazes threatened those who may enter with ill intentions.

Like the real Ra, the statues' eyes were wary. Though his powers and skills in battle overshadowed all other gods, he bore an unhealthy obsession with the fear of being overthrown. It was as though he might suspect a dagger at his back, or a lie upon his servants' lips always, though neither concern seemed justifiable. He was consumed by thoughts of losing his throne, which is also why he appointed Bastet—a willing bodyguard. I wondered if the people of Egypt realized how very anxious and preoccupied Ra was with his own wellbeing, if they would avert their beliefs?

Who was I to stand before a sacred place and commit

such blasphemy?

Ra would separate me from what little power he had granted, had he known the thoughts that flashed across my mind, even as briefly as lightning.

A rustle of footsteps distracted me, and I raised my eyes toward the walkway leading inside the temple. Young girls dressed in white scrambled about, gathering flowers from baskets left as contributions from villagers and tossing petals across the path. Some were still children, but a few were of child-bearing age. Fresh. Innocent. Pure in heart and manner. They had all clearly been chosen for their youth and chastity. Each had an aura about them that defined them as those who had married their faith, quite literally.

No other god possessed such elegant, dedicated shrines as Amun Ra. The female-only disciples at his temples—each called a God's Wife—had been individually chosen to spend the rest of their lives worshipping only one.

Bastet had briefly mentioned them before, though I had thought them to be myths, at the time. A god is forbidden to show affection toward, or to favor a mortal, so why would they expect such behavior in return from the humans?

Once inducted into service, because they were wives of the King of the Gods, Ra, it was forbidden for any human male to touch them. No exceptions were to be made or they would be considered tarnished and impure—unfit to serve the Pharaoh God.

Seeing the fair, delicate young girls scurrying around—some porting offerings inside the temple, while others diligently swept sand from the walkways—made me wonder what temptations had been offered to them that would make them consider embracing such a lackluster fate.

Some baskets left contained rare foods and fruits, and, seeing that the state of the public was in constant fluctuation, one could suppose the occupation allowed them to live without worry of starvation. Perhaps giving up the freedom to take a mortal husband and to live as they pleased was a small price to pay for the assurance of health and longevity.

In the few moments that I stood watching them, I could already tell these girls were treated like princesses. People offered them nourishing food, clean water, fine clothing, and respect. In a sense, they were Earth-bound goddesses seen as liaisons between the common man and the immortal Ra.

I flinched as a townswoman walked straight through me; I was an apparition to them. My attention had been locked onto the others and I had not noticed her coming. She carried a tiny babe swaddled in cotton, with its face shielded loosely from the harsh morning rays.

A very young God's Wife met her at the entrance and smiled. "Have you brought a child for blessing?" she asked in a mousey voice.

"May I speak with Head Priestess Zahra?" the woman asked.

The girl nodded, set down her basket of flowers, and then turned and hurried inside.

"Your aunt will be here soon, my little star," said the mother to her babe. The head priestess God's Wife, Zahra, her name meaning 'white flower,' must have been her sister.

Moments later, a young woman with her face covered by a white veil exited the shrine and walked toward the pair.

"Good morning, Khepri," Zahra said, her airy voice

nearly a whisper. "I hope Taweret was kind to you in childbirth."

Khepri, her name one of many representing the morning sun, could not contain her excitement and hastily uncovered the infant's face.

"It is a boy!" she chirped, beaming with joy. "He is just as I had prayed he would be."

The God's Wife recoiled and muttered, "That is good news, Sister," as she began to back away. All anticipation had vanished from her expression and worry swept across her face.

"Please, Zahra, will you bless him so that he will grow to be strong and healthy? Grant my dear boy the protection of our Lord Amun Ra. We would ask the favor of no one but you." Khepri held the boy out toward her sister, but Zahra turned her back and shuddered.

"I can not," she replied, her gaze sweeping the floor and shifting nervously behind her veil. "I have sworn myself to Ra, and I have made the unbreakable oath to not touch another man in my lifetime—to remain chaste and devoted to my husband."

Khepri's voice wavered. "B-but... Sister... you—"

"By marrying a mortal man, you made the decision to bind yourself to a life of servitude and motherhood, while I swore to deprive myself of the touch of a man." She swallowed hard and sighed. "Even if that bars me from blessing your infant son."

"He is but a babe!" Khepri's eyes welled with tears and she reached out to grab her sister by the shoulder, still hugging the infant close to her chest. "Please!"

"With the gods willing, your son will become a strong, healthy man," Zahra replied, jerking her arm from her sister's grasp.

With my falcon sight, I could see through feeble barriers, and I saw tears glistening in her eyes, hidden by her veil. Her lip trembled and she sucked in a distressed breath, trying to keep her feelings from her sister. "I am sorry, Sister, but I cannot grant your infant the blessing he requires. Take him to the temple of Isis; someone there will perform the ritual for you without conflict."

The God's Wife shook her head and retreated back inside the temple. I followed behind her, glancing back once to witness Khepri fall to her knees and hug her newborn close, weeping heavily.

Inside Ra's temple, there were tables and shelves displaying perfumed oils, candles, golden plates for offerings, and various stone idols. A trough ran about the perimeter of the massive entry room, with channels leading up and outside, which were meant to catch and store rainwater.

Zahra retrieved one of the trays with a mirror-like finish and side-stepped to the perfume jars nearby. Her fingers hovered over them for several moments as she diligently decided which to choose. She selected one and plucked it from the shelf. Next, she reached below the table and procured a feather duster. Lastly, she gathered a small bowl, which she filled with clean rainwater, and a loaf of bread from one of the offering baskets.

Each item was carefully arranged on the golden tray so that no two items touched, and everything had been lined up in a perfectly straight row. She lifted the tray from the table with both hands and carried it into a softly lit room tucked away to the back and off to the side of the main space.

This darker room had no windows and only a walkway lined with candles leading the way to the foot of another statue of Ra. Smaller than those at the entryway, this one had been carved sitting on a throne, straight and dignified, and was adorned with gold leaf and rare gemstones.

I stood beside the candlelit walkway and watched as Zahra took a bow at the threshold of the room. She then entered, bowed again, set the tray down in front of the statue, and knelt onto her hands and knees. She lowered her head to the floor and remained silent for several minutes.

After a deep inhalation, she slowly rose and sat back on her heels.

Zahra lifted the feather brush from the golden tray and used it to whisk away dust and sand from Ra's feet. She put it back, quite precisely, into place, and lifted the bowl of water high over her head, as if to gain his permission to use it, before pouring it slowly and tenderly across the statue's feet. After returning the empty bowl to the tray, she retrieved the perfume bottle. She plucked the stopper from the top and dipped two fingers into the oil.

With her smooth, youthful hands, she proceeded to rub oil between the statue's toes, applying a potent fragrance of herbs and flowers to the 'skin.'

It was often considered the wife's duty to keep her husband's body clean and purified, but I had never imagined this type of behavior would take place between a mortal and a statue.

An inkling of frustration and anger sparked inside me,

knowing that such immaculate devotion had almost certainly gone unnoticed by Ra, for he did not pay heed to the prayers of individuals. He had made clear to us all that his council of 'servants' was to toil with trivial matters, while he managed what he claimed were 'more important' ones.

Zahra placed the stopper back into the perfume bottle, put it aside, and gazed up into Ra's never-changing stone face. Alone in her worship, as head priestess of the temple, there were no others there to witness what she did next. She lifted her veil up over her face and let it fall back against her neck.

Her skin was a shade fairer than others I had seen in the city, and it was obvious she rarely left the temple or felt the sun's rays. Deep red stain tinted her lips with vivid, blood-like color, and her eyelids, glittered with radiant blue, reflected the candlelight. Beaded strands of black hair fell in front of her shoulders and large golden hoop earrings clinked as she lowered her face back to the ground and kissed the stone before Ra's feet.

Like a candlewick, something ignited in me; a deep, visceral spark twisted and churned in the pit of my soul, filling me with an unusual sense of concern for this... mortal.

Witnessing her unwavering faith in the presence of an infant and seeing her graceful act of undying devotion toward a lifeless statue imbued me with a revelation.

This God's Wife, Zahra, was rare and beautiful—too exquisite to be the wife of a god who would not witness her faith or loyalty even once during her fleeting lifetime.

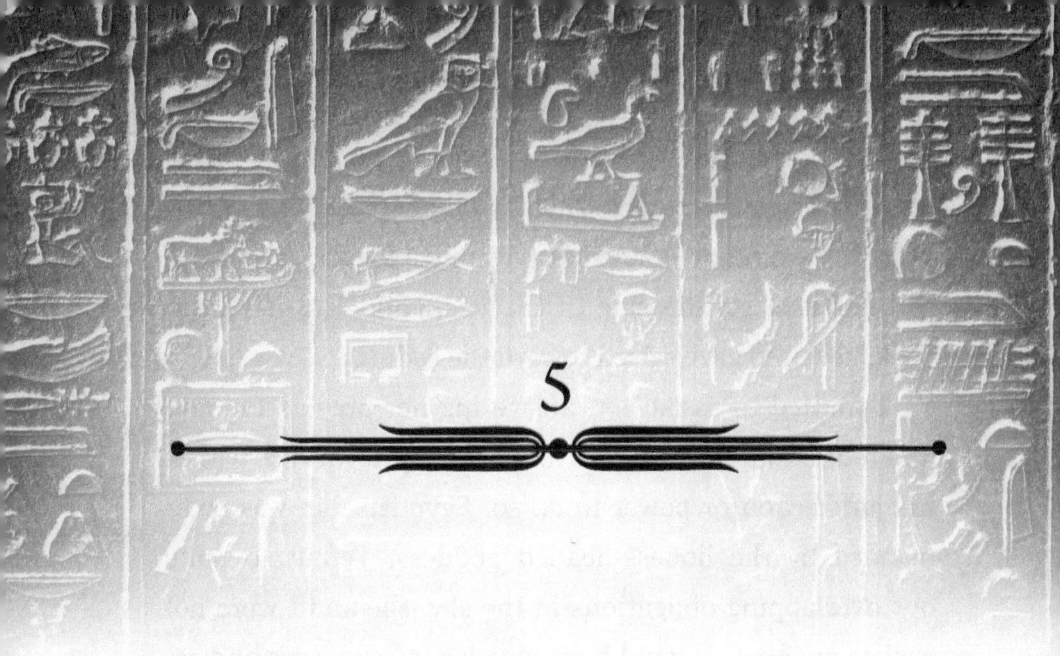

5

The Oath of the Gods

None shall alter one's fate.
None shall favor another.
None shall undo others' work.
None shall cause death.
None shall grant life to the dead.

Zahra cupped water in her hands and splashed it onto her face. She wiped sweat from her brow and then used a clean cloth to pat her forehead and cheeks. The head priestess struggled with the stifling air and fierce afternoon sun but hid her discomfort from the other God's Wives. She sat in a small side room inside the temple, across from the central shrine to Ra, at which she had been praying earlier.

The interior channels of rainwater had begun to evaporate, and there was talk amongst the villagers of her god's disapproval looming.

"Please grant us some relief from your temper, my lord,"

she whispered, heaving a breath as she tugged at the fabric of her dress, which stuck uncomfortably to her perspiring skin. “We cannot tolerate your rage much longer.” She dropped her arm off the side of the chair and laid her head back, her tired gaze raised toward the ceiling.

I wanted to assist her, answering her prayers for rain and relief from Ra’s overbearing heat, but it was not within my jurisdiction or power to do so. Egyptian rain was commanded by the lioness-headed goddess, Tefnut. Despite our overlapping obligations in the sky, she and I were not well acquainted. I would have to voice my concerns and requests to the goddess directly if I wanted rain to fall; however, I did not require her permission to bring the clouds together to provide some shelter from Ra’s burning gaze.

“Ra will not answer your prayers, Zahra,” I said, approaching her until I stood within arm’s length. She could not see nor hear me, though I could see the individual beads of sweat glistening on her cheeks. “But I will.”

I concentrated on the air in the room, focusing every bit of my essence into willing the temperature to change. A flicker of breeze swirled around Zahra’s chair, making the hem of her skirt dance at her ankles, though there were no windows in the room. Startled, she gasped, jolted from her seat, and looked around.

“Come, Zahra,” I whispered as I backed away, even though she still could not hear me. She instinctively followed my gentle, cooling aura outside, into the blazing afternoon sunlight. She squinted and raised a hand to her brow.

At the archway of the temple, I strained to summon every glint of my magic as I looked toward the clouds. I raised my arms out to my sides and reached up to pluck the shallow tufts of milky white from the backdrop of blue.

In childish fantasies, I had imagined myself swiping clouds away with a snap of my fingers, but it was not so easy now. It felt as though I commanded a chariot of a hundred horses with reins pulled taut, and the effort swiftly depleted my strength.

My feebleness made me feel ashamed.

The God of the Sky should be more powerful than this.

I should be more powerful.

My jaw tightened and I struggled to keep my arms up, focusing everything into my fingertips and up to the clouds, but the harder I tried, the slower they moved, crawling toward each other like inchworms on muddy ground.

Zahra began to withdraw back inside the temple and the sight of her slipping away sent a coil of rage pulsing through me. Switching my attention from the entire sky to a smaller patch of clouds overhead, I thrust my hands together and held my breath as the puff of white began to inch toward the sun, slowly causing the golden light to dim until a shadow had been cast upon the temple.

I let out a sigh of relief and shook my head with disappointment. Who would I fool with these trivial acts of magic? Certainly not the wise, wary people of Egypt.

I lowered my eyes to the ground and closed them. Zahra remained nearby, her face turned toward the sky.

"Thank you," she uttered.

An unfamiliar tingle of energy coursed through me, surrounding me in a flurry of strange, but pleasurable sensations. Warm, yellow light emanated from beneath my skin, and a dusting of bright golden sparkles tickled my fingertips.

The amulet around my neck suddenly felt heavier; I lifted up the large gemstone so that I could examine the piece as it twinkled faintly. Through the mask Bastet had cast over its damaged exterior, I witnessed a small portion of the crack fading back into solid stone.

The amulet was healing...

"It will become whole again, in time," a familiar voice spoke from behind me. I turned to find Bastet approaching. "Continue to nurture your powers and benefit the mortals and you will realize your true potential."

"So I *can* gain my destiny on my own, then?" I asked, a smile curling my lips. "I need not wait for Ra to grant it to me?"

"We gods are powerless without mortal faith," Bastet added. "Ra is our lord not only because he has captured the devotion of the humans, but also because he has garnered that of all the gods. Without mortals, there are no immortals. Without us, there is no king."

"What a fragile system," I replied.

"Fragile, indeed, Horus. It is why you must make the most of your time here in the city. The lifetime of a single mortal can pass in the blink of a god's eye."

How could one rule a race with such short life spans and still build empathy and rapport with them? It made very little sense to me.

"As immortals, we are forced to care from afar," Bastet clarified. "Love without loving and serve without becoming a servant."

A delicate balance, I suppose.

"It will come to you with experience and time," she

continued. “Are you returning to the palace soon?”

“Soon, yes.”

“I will see you then.” She acknowledged my words and then faded from sight.

I turned back to the entrance of Ra’s temple, only to find Zahra on her knees beside it, praying and giving thanks for the cloud cover. There were no other God’s Wives in the vicinity. I approached her and came down onto one knee.

“It was not Ra who granted this brief salvation from the heat,” I began. “It was I, Horus—God of the Sky.”

She lifted her head slightly and sucked in a quick breath, her eyes widened as if she had heard my words very far in the back of her mind.

With an open hand close to my lips, I blew a puff of air lightly at her face. The cool wisp sifting through her hair made her smile, even as she tugged her veil down so that it would not be pulled away.

Zahra seemed very modest, but then I did not know the extent of human modesty, so I did not know who to compare her to. She seemed, to me, to be very reserved with her body and words. I had seen the way she reacted to her newborn nephew. All in the name of her faith.

Before leaving the temple to return to the Palace of the Gods, I pleaded briefly to the rain goddess, Tefnut, to allow the clouds to stay in place for a little longer on this harsh afternoon. I also asked that she consider a sprinkling of rain, were she not too busy to oblige.

It was apparently a trifle of a favor to ask of the grand rain goddess, and she was bewildered by my request, but accommodating. She promised a fleeting drizzle in the late evening. I thanked her for it and returned to the palace.

Back in my empty room, I rested in a chair and allowed the result of my day to settle in.

The new power I had gained continued to pulse through me, making me yearn for more. I had had a taste of magic and the power of mortal faith, and I hungered for it.

At the far side of my room stood a gold and gemstone encrusted mirror. The sparkling crystals surrounding it had been extracted from tears wept by the goddess Nut, and it had the rare ability to reflect one's true self and to foresee the future. It would show me not only my current form, but visions of the god I desired to become.

When I approached the mirror, the face of a falcon and the extravagant wings I eagerly awaited glistened as a mirage overlapping my body.

Intricate, brightly colored feathers flowed down my shoulders and back. My amulet was completely restored. The details were so vivid and clear, and yet so far from my grasp.

But then pomegranate-red-stained lips flashed through my memory, shattering the illusion.

Zahra?

I had seen over a thousand faces in the past few days on Earth, but hers—with her vivid blue eye shadow, reserved voice, carefully performed ceremonial service, and impenetrable devout faith—had stayed with me.

It was forged in the Oath of the Gods that one shall not favor another, but the feelings rushing through me defied all reason. I did not understand the sudden urge to go—right then—back to the Temple of Ra to visit her again, so soon.

The craving was foreign and complicated.

I may have been one of the youngest gods in the palace, but I still had my wits about me. A single mortal human should not have been able to influence me. There were thousands of sheep in my flock, and I was to watch over them all with equal diligence.

But her image remained in my mind, as crisp and clear as if she stood beside me before the mirror.

I recalled the way she had treated the feet of the shrine statue—passionately, her hands moving deliberately and precisely, as if lost in a spell. I remembered the way her veil hid her exquisite face from others.

Perhaps the ignorant and dangerous idea of how I might steal her away from the Temple of Ra so that she might worship only me had passed through my mind. Perhaps I wished for her to wash my feet so tenderly, and that she might reveal her face to me alone.

For a moment, the desire for power that burned brightly in my chest and beat so loudly from my heart had shifted into a desire for something even further from my grasp—Zahra's touch.

6

"**THAT is** why Lord Ra must take many forms during his battles against the dark serpent, Apep, so that he may prevent him from devouring the sun."

Zahra closed her book and set it down beside the smallest, youngest God's Wife, Nephiri, who lay beside the other wives on a straw mat on the floor.

A benefit of being the high priestess of the Temple of Ra allowed Zahra the privilege to learn to read and write. Only she could read stories to the other wives, and only she could recite and teach prayers from the scriptures of the gods.

"Sleep well," Zahra spoke softly to the child. "Ra has defeated Apep and will recover here until morning."

She pulled a beige linen sheet up to Nephiri's shoulder and stroked her hand over her head, ruffling the little girl's hair playfully. "Goodnight, all," she added, standing from the floor and excusing herself to return to her private bedchamber—an additional advantage of being head priestess.

I followed.

Zahra sat upon a small, simple cot, which was low to the

ground and made of wood. The bedding consisted of cotton and wool fibers stuffed into a linen casing, set atop palm boughs, and she appeared to be quite comfortable upon it.

One by one, she removed her jasper and quartz bracelets. Next were her golden anklets, then her large hoop earrings, and lastly her beaded carnelian necklace. She placed them all into a small wooden box beside her cot. Then she slid her linen shawl from her back, exposing her shoulders to the night air, and hung it on a bedpost.

A small bowl of water was nearby; she dipped a cloth into it, rung it out, and wiped it over her face, removing the colored shadow and black kohl from her eyes. Then she dropped the soiled cloth back into the water and reached down to remove her leather sandals.

Zahra massaged her feet for awhile, as if it were a nightly ritual, and groaned quietly to herself, as the act seemed both relaxing and difficult. After stretching her legs and flexing her toes, she tucked them under a thin linen sheet and sat back against her pillow.

She removed her veil, set it aside, and then turned to knead her old, flat pillow until it was to her liking. She wriggled under her sheet and laid her head down.

All this work for sleep?

It made me thankful gods did not have to partake in such arduous endeavors. We could rest if we chose to, between certain phases of the sun, but we did not need to. Not like humans did.

This allowed us to remain ever vigilant.

And it allowed me to stay awake while Zahra slept.

I sat on the edge of her bed, without her even knowing,

and watched her dream. When her eyelids twitched, I touched her forehead with the tip of my index finger and saw what she was seeing—the miracle of clouds drawing before the sun and providing relief to her earlier in the day. *My* miracle.

But as the hours withered away, her dreams began to seize and torment her, making her tremble and causing a stream of tears to drizzle down her cheeks. I touched her forehead again, to interpret the vision, and a blast of violent imagery tore through my mind—a flash of vivid red and a piercing shriek. I was sent reeling from her consciousness, rattled and confused, unable to comprehend what she had seen.

Was that... pain? I could not tell. Whatever it was, it made my skin tingle and my heartbeat quicken. It was uncomfortable and foreign, and I wanted no part of it.

But Zahra continued to sob in her sleep, and I did not know how to ease her suffering.

Then I recalled what Bastet had done for me after Ra had mortified me before the council of the gods, and how a simple touch and a few kind words were able to give me back my courage.

I rested a hand on Zahra's bare shoulder, leaned closer, and whispered, "You are safe. There is nothing to fear in the night while you are under my protection."

Her trembling ceased.

She turned her head upwards, her eyes still closed, and asked, "Who are you?"

I knew she could not see me, though I wished she might, if only to assure her of my presence.

"I am Horus, God of the Sky," I replied, "the light which

will protect you from the darkness that threatens your slumber."

Her breaths slowly began to return to normal, becoming deeper and longer, as she fell back into a peaceful sleep. Then my gaze rose to her face again and lingered there, tracing the curves of her high, defined cheekbones, and drifting down toward her mauve lips, and then to her sharp chin.

To think she would shield such a beautiful face from the world each day, while the other God's Wives did not, was perplexing. For modesty's sake alone, it seemed impractical, at least while there were those of us gods who found pleasure in looking upon her.

"You are beautiful, Zahra," I said, glancing toward the side of her bed, to where she had placed her veil. "You need not shield your face." With a flick of my hand, I sent the cloth into the wind, out of the temple and into the distant land, where she would never find it.

Bastet had warned me to keep my distance from the mortals, but I sensed a strong connection with Zahra, which I could not ignore. Different. Free. Freer than I had ever felt in the Palace of the Gods. Bastet had also added that the humans could not know us... What a petty rule!

She had told me herself that we gods are nothing without the faith of our people. How can we rely on them and be expected to turn a blind eye to their turmoil?

Zahra stirred again in her sleep, but it was fleeting. Experiencing another brief flash of her nightmare did not make me feel strong and omnipotent, as a god should feel, but transparent and fragile. I would live a thousand lifetimes beyond Zahra's, but her brevity and depth made her invaluable. Despite the fact that gods are imbued with magic and the ability to sway the tides and man's destiny, mortal flaws gave humans uniqueness and rarity.

Their opaque skin is imperfect and scarred, freckled and weathered by labor and the elements. Hands wrinkled. Feet calloused. Eyes weary. Their clothing, unlike pristine garments worn by gods, is soiled and in constant need of mending. It is temporary and cannot withstand the everyday endeavors of wives and farmers, merchants and soldiers.

Humans shed blood. Gods do not. We cannot die a mortal death. If our ka abandons us, we vanish into oblivion. I do not even know what pain is, or why it causes a mortal face to crease and change so violently when it is experienced, though the vision from Zahra's dream had offered me a glimpse.

A deep, visceral sensation filled me with discomfort and I stood from her bed. I craned my neck; my gaze could cut through stone, allowing me to see Ra drawing up the sun, and that my time with Zahra was coming to an end. I would have to return to my duties.

The grand ibises commenced in their morning flight over the city, loud nasally shrieks resonating across the village as they flew.

Just then, Zahra sat up on her bed with a start and looked around as if she had heard something. "Is someone there?" she asked, her eyes darting from wall to wall.

I sensed the sky calling to me, but I waited.

After a few moments, Zahra dressed and adorned herself with jewelry. I waited until she reapplied her makeup and adjusted her hair. She put on her sandals, her shawl, and then...

"My veil? Where is it?" she asked, checking below her cot and then around her nearby table. She skimmed the perimeter of her room. Finally, she bent down, stretched her arm under her bed, and withdrew it with another veil in hand.

I scowled.

"You will not cover your face," I repeated, though she could not hear me. Then I curled my fingers inward and forced the second cloth from her grasp. She chased after it as it flew from her room into the next, and then gasped as I sent it soaring out the main entrance and into the sky.

She stopped at the threshold of the temple and peered out, watching as the ivory veil was whisked away by the breeze and danced across the horizon until it disappeared into a blur.

"The sky is beautiful this morning," said the youngest wife, Nephiri, coming up behind Zahra and startling her. "Ra is smiling."

Zahra hesitantly turned to greet the girl, looking away shyly and raising a hand in a poor attempt to cover her face.

Nephiri flicked her ebony bangs away from her brow and gawked back at the head priestess. "You are very beautiful, too!" she said excitedly. "Oh, your face is so very pretty. Mother Isis has surely granted you her beauty."

Zahra could not help but smile, and in doing so, she lowered her hand down to her side.

"Thank you, little one," she said. "Now please go wake the other wives, so that we may begin our duties."

Nephiri nodded and left the room with a skip in her step.

Zahra stood in the doorway, staring up at the sky. Tears began to fill her eyes, reflecting the colors of dawn.

"I am not strong enough," she muttered, shuffling back to her room. I followed after her, watching as she flung herself upon her bed and started to cry. "I cannot face them this way."

I did not understand her outburst, so I watched, vainly, never having felt so ignorant.

She cupped her face with her hands and her eyes and cheeks reddened.

I had assumed the veil was an aesthetic choice alone, but it was clear to me now that she *needed* it.

"I..." I approached her bedside and knelt. "Zahra..." My words fell upon deaf ears, but I spoke them anyway. "Please, do not be ashamed of your face. Your veil did not define you as a devoted priestess or God's Wife. Only your faith may define who you are." I placed a hand on her shoulder; faint sparks of golden energy emanated from my fingertips, twinkling and casting a warm glow against her skin.

She sucked in a sharp breath and lifted her face from her pillow, her brows furrowing and her jaw easing open. She sat up and wiped her face with the back of her hands, smudging eye shadow across her palms and temples.

"I must be strong," she said, sniffling again. "A God's Wife must be strong."

I stood and took a step back as she got up from her bed and retrieved the cloth from the water bowl. She used it to pat her face, reducing some of the redness, and then gathered her makeup and a small silver reflective plate, and diligently and swiftly restored the vibrant colors to her eyelids.

"You *are* strong," I whispered, standing behind her, though I cast no reflection in her mirror.

A small, humble smile stretched across her face as she gazed at herself.

"I *am* strong," she repeated.

Had she heard me?

Exuding new confidence, she shook out her dress, rolled her shoulders back, and then made her way to the main hall to greet the other wives.

If I could convince a dedicated woman like Zahra to release her inhibitions and reveal her face to the world, though she did not want to, then surely I could face the tribulations of regaining my powers.

Her courage renewed my own.

7

I RETURNED to the Palace of the Gods, to an unwelcome visitor lounging in my chamber—my estranged uncle, and Ra's confidant, Set. He slunk off my bed and then brushed at his cloak with his bony, grey fingers. Flecks of red and white magic glittered along the fabric and emitted a disconcerting hum.

As a child, I had been told stories about Set's cloak, how it had been woven from threads painstakingly harvested in the abyss of souls—a stagnate, inky pool of forsaken kas gathered from warriors who had begged for Set's blessing in battle. He was a devious god, and by making such a pact, those souls relinquished their chance at rebirth or peace in the underworld, while fueling Set's unorthodox ways of collecting magic.

"How fares my *favorite* nephew?" Set's voice was low and gruff, like a landslide, crackling as he spoke. I despised it. Immortality had been cruel to him; his body was frail and in a constant state of atrophy, with ashen skin and muscles so weak, they clung to his bones like wet linen.

"What do you want, Uncle?" I asked, though I had no desire to hear him.

He approached me and smiled; his long, deformed canine snout curved downward like a scythe and wrinkled awkwardly when he grinned.

In an effort to deceive adversaries, he had lopped off the tops of his ears, making them flat, and then cauterized them with embers so that they could not reveal his true intentions. He used self-mutilation to alter his appearance, and while I had been belittled for my harmless change of face achieved with simple magic, Ra had had no complaints about Set's actions. He had even declared him the god of thunder and, fittingly, chaos.

Ra looked to Set for all manners of advice, and in return, he offered Set the governance of all Upper Egypt. Lower Egypt would eventually fall under my jurisdiction—once I had acquired all my godly powers. The Temple of Ra, where Zahra resided, could be found precisely at the border line of both lands; the thought of her falling into Set's manipulative hands made me uneasy.

"Are you having trouble with your powers, Horus?" he asked, lowering his head to peer into my shattered amulet. His vivid yellow eyes focused intently, following the fractures through the stone and then rising to meet my gaze. "Oh, my! What a serious problem."

There was deep-rooted disdain in my heart for Set, because he hated my father, and thus I hated him. Osiris fairly won custody and control over the underworld by defeating Set in a battle of wits. My grandparents, Nut and Geb (the goddess of the stars, and her husband, the creator of Earth) challenged their children to a riddle. Uncle Set allowed his impatience to get the best of him, and he incorrectly solved the puzzle, allowing his brother, Osiris, to be crowned king of the underworld. My mother, Isis, wished for us all to get along, but the differences between us were like dawn and dusk. Light and shadow.

"I do not require your assistance," I said, backing away from him. He was much taller than me, but shorter than Ra.

"Why so angry, boy? I have come here because I sensed your distress. I only wish to help."

"I am no longer a boy, Uncle. I can find my own way."

Set narrowed his eyes at me and reached up to flick a lock of my hair from my brow with his sharp claws. I flinched, certain his nail had grazed my flesh, though the sensation was fleeting.

"A young, inexperienced god requires an exceptional mentor. Do you not agree?"

I scoffed. "I *will* find my own way. Please, leave me."

"As you wish, young Horus," he hissed, his long purple tongue flitting between his teeth as he spoke. "But I advise you to do away with that pitiful human mask. It is unbecoming of the Sky God."

"We are worshipped by '*pitiful*' humans," I replied. "Your lack of respect for them is 'unbecoming of a god.'"

Set's eyes narrowed, but his pupils grew larger, his gaze darkening with frustration.

"We are finished here, Uncle." I lifted my chin and pointed toward the threshold. "Leave." I would not allow him to intimidate me.

With a muffled snarl and an agitated wrinkle of his lips,

which he hid unsuccessfully from my falcon sight, he turned and shuffled out of the room, his hauntingly beautiful cloak sweeping across the floor and vanishing with him.

Set had no business pestering me about my powers; he did not know what I would soon be capable of, and I did not require his help.

I lifted my hand and waved it through the air, willing a wall of my chamber to fade and reveal the parted clouds and pristine River Nile below. From my room, I could look down onto the cities of Egypt and weave my magic without having to leave.

But I *wanted* to leave.

Despite its splendor and sanctity, the Palace of the Gods did not grant me a sense of belonging. Something I had learned quickly from Zahra, after I had stolen her precious veil away, was that humans had the ability to make their own choices—for better or worse. She decided how to pursue her faith, as would I.

I peered over the edge of my room and down at the specks of dust—temples and homes. There were responsibilities out there for me to take hold of and it was time I accepted them.

I leapt over the edge and down toward the earth, diving with greater speed and agility than I had before. My body had become stronger, and I possessed great power and control, leading me to realize something: although childish fantasies had made me long for them, the truth was that *I did not need wings to fly*.

I soared across the sky, through wispy clouds, toward the river below. The seasons were changing, and a great variety of birds migrated here from foreign lands to avoid the hazards of cold weather. My position as Sky God meant that I was now responsible for assuring their safe passage and granting them a warm reception. Since childhood, I had studied maps and migration patterns meticulously, as it was my duty to shift the air currents to facilitate their flights and guide the birds to safety.

I rotated my hands and curled my fingers, manipulating and drawing the air currents into patterns necessary for the arriving geese and other waterfowl. Birds shifted their wings like steering oars on a ship, twisting midair and coming to gentle landings in the water.

I assisted a flock of ducks next, and they landed along the banks of the glistening river, their feathers gleaming with gemlike flashes of emerald and copper.

As I watched a pair of regal ibises wade through the water, hunting for fish, my thoughts were invaded by visions of Zahra once more. Glimpses of her ivory dress and scarlet accents distracted me from my duties, and I tried to force them from my mind. I could not push out the memory of her rich brown eyes.

With my migration duties finished for the time being, I ventured back to the Temple of Ra.

A great many more offerings had been left; food, decanters of fresh water, flowers, small sculptures, and scrolls surrounded the temple.

The great bird migrations brought many visitors to the cities and the marketplace swelled with bustling crowds and tourists.

The wives of Ra were busy greeting patrons and bringing

offerings inside the temple, so I decided it would be better to return at dusk, once my own day had been completed and my presence no longer required by the other gods.

8

Oil lamp flames danced to hymns whispered by the evening breeze, illuminating stones and chasing off shadows around the Temple of Ra. All the day's offerings had finally been brought in, and Zahra had stepped outside to extinguish the lights. The other God's Wives had returned inside and were performing a final ceremony for the night before they would retire to sleep.

Seeing Zahra without her veil made me smile. She was thriving without it, and an aura of tranquility and joy resonated around her. I watched as she approached each lamp, bent slowly, and then snuffed out the wick. One by one, each flame was put to rest. When she reached the final one, which flitted bravely against the wind, she reached down to lift the lamp into her hands and began to walk back toward the main temple archway, using it to guide her way in the darkness.

A horrendous yowl rang out, followed by a ferocious hiss. In the distant shadows, I saw a pair of cats tumbling about in a vicious fight. A scuffle in the sand sent one of them darting away, and a chase ensued. Before she could turn to see what the commotion was, Zahra was struck in the leg by one of the running cats, and she fumbled to maintain her grasp on the lamp. As she regained her balance and cupped the lit lantern tightly, the second cat plowed into her and she toppled to the ground.

A blaze of fire consumed the hem of her dress and chased the scattered oil stain toward her waist. She yelped in pain and patted her dress frantically, trying to put out the flames as they ravaged her linen skirt, searing her ankles.

The cats disappeared into the night, but the fire continued to rage, even as the priestess reeled on the ground. I lifted both arms and forced my hands toward her, willing sand and wind to rise and smother the flames.

But nothing happened, and the sand remained unresponsive. Zahra's painful cries continued to sting my ears as she writhed in agony. Fears for her safety compelled me to try again. This time, I lifted my fingers higher and focused on drawing together *all* my magic. I thrust my hands out again, grunting as a rush of energy shot through my body, making me bite down. A gust of wind swept up around her and a wave of sand draped over her legs, quelling the deadly light.

She panted and strained to come to her knees, just as two other God's Wives came out to check on her.

"What happened, Zahra?" one asked, reaching an arm out to her.

She came to her feet and doubled over, out of breath.

"Your dress!" The other wife looked down at the singed fabric. "Are you hurt?"

Zahra pushed away from them, stumbling back into the temple and demanding they not follow. She hurried past the threshold of her room, staggering on painful legs, and then took a seat on her cot and pulled her feet up onto the soft pile of cotton and palm boughs.

She leaned to the side and craned her neck to look at her ankles, slowly drawing up her charred, crumbling skirt with her hands. A muffled whimper escaped her lips and she grimaced, revealing a large patch of inflamed, blistered skin. The burns ran from her ankle, up her calf, and toward her knee, more apparent on one leg than the other. Touching them with the tip of her finger sent her reeling back. Tears glistened in her eyes and she began to weep.

I watched her cry, unsure of how I might alleviate her pain. Then I glanced up, toward the Palace of the Gods, and whispered, "Why?"

Why did Ra not show compassion and dedication to his mortal servants? "She is in pain," I continued, looking again at the bright red, bubbling, scalded wound on Zahra's leg. I shook my head. "You care as much for your people as you do for your fellow gods."

Zahra reached to the side of her bed for the water bowl and clutched onto the wet cloth drifting at the bottom. She squeezed it out and inched it closer to her wound. A low, painful murmur resonated from her throat as she pressed the damp rag against the wound, clenching her teeth and struggling to keep her voice down.

I quickly approached, leaned down, and pressed a hand over hers. Pale light illuminated my fingertips and faded into her skin. She gasped, and then fell silent.

Zahra held her breath and leaned back against her pillow. She released the wet cloth and wiped her eyes with her hands. It slid to the floor, and she shrieked.

The blisters had vanished, revealing smooth, pristine skin.

I drew back my arm, surprised my spell had actually worked as I had intended.

Her face lifted and her eyes scanned the room. Briefly, our gazes met and a tinge of discomfort coiled in my stomach.

She could not see me, could she?

No.

There was no way she could—

"Thank you," she whispered.

I stiffened from shock.

Had she known I was there? How!?

"I do not know who you are, but you have my gratitude." Her voice rose, but she continued to speak in a hushed tone.

Wait...

She did not think I was Ra?

Why would a God's Wife believe any god other than her own would come to her aid?

Zahra shook out her skirt and brushed it down against her knees.

"I must get this mended," she uttered, looking quite embarrassed, though she should not have; she had nearly lost her life.

A hand rose and she brushed a braid of hair behind her ear. "I apologize for speaking of trivial worries." She looked up toward the wall, past me. "I know that you are not my husband." Her voice softened again, but my sharp ears heard her clearly. "I have been Ra's wife for many years; I have faced many tribulations, but I have never been granted such sympathy."

She reached up toward her neck and slid one shoulder strap of her dress off, revealing a large, raised oval scar on her back, just above her shoulder blade.

"When I was admitted into the temple as a child, chosen to become head priestess, I was struck by an arrow." Her fingers slid across the old wound. "There were those who did not believe I could please their god, and one cruel person made their opinion known." She slid the strap back up over her shoulder and dropped her head. "The villagers believed I would bleed to death, because I was young and—at the time—very frail. But they were wrong, and I survived, though it was a slow and painful recovery wrought with infection and fever.

"My god was not at my side then... and I fear he is not at my side now." Her face rose and she looked around the room again, searching for me.

"Please, tell me who you are," she whispered, a subtle smile tugging at her lips.

I had wanted to speak to her so that she might hear me, but it was forbidden, so I remained silent.

Several moments of silence passed.

"If you cannot tell me, then show me. I swear to never speak of it."

The urge to reveal myself to her *somehow* was clawing at me, challenging me to find a way—any way—to make myself known. But Bastet had warned me that the humans must not know us. Still, I desired for Zahra, Ra's head priestess and wife, to know who had shown her kindness.

An idea struck me, and I approached her again, focusing my magic on drawing her hand up and out toward me. She appeared bewildered by her involuntary movements but did not seem fearful as her hand lifted and turned, revealing her bare wrist, by my command.

With my index finger, I began to trace a shape upon her flesh, and she closed her eyes as if in a trance.

First, a thin oval on its side.

Next, a gently curving horizontal line hovering across the top.

I pressed a large dot into the center of the oval with my thumb, and then drew a short line straight down from there, and another which went from the center dot down and to the left, at a diagonal, and curled at the tip.

I wrapped my fingers around her wrist, grasped it tightly for a moment, and then let go.

She opened her eyes and sucked in a breath.

"The eye of Ra?" She examined the darkened skin closely. "No. It is different and... it faces the opposite direction." As she sat pondering the origin and meaning of the tattoo, I withdrew a red strip of linen from a nearby bin and sent it floating over to her. It drifted down onto her lap.

"I understand." She nodded. "I will keep it our secret." She grasped the red cloth, twirled it around her wrist, and twisted the ends together into a careful knot. Then she clasped her hand around it and glanced down at her ankle. "Thank you, again."

Another wave of white light roiled beneath my skin, the

new magic tingling in my veins. It took me a moment to realize that I was smiling again. It pleased me greatly to know that I had gained the respect of the head priestess of Ra.

But in the far corners of my mind, the truth threatened me—it was blasphemous to convert a follower of Ra, especially a sacred God's Wife.

At the same time, the fresh energy coursing through me conveyed a deep sense of purpose.

It was worth the risk.

"Will you return to see me?" she asked softly.

I brought my fingers to her cheek and she closed her eyes as if she could feel them there.

"Yes, Zahra," I replied; she could not hear me.

9

DAWN approached and Ra harnessed his horses in preparation for his morning crusade against the colossal serpent, Apep, who had once again slithered into the horizon in an attempt to devour the sun.

I sat in my chamber, awaiting the chance to start my day, knowing it was dependant upon Ra's victory against the beast, but confident he would triumph because it was preordained.

Just as I was destined to become the Sky God.

The mark I had given Zahra was a variation of the eye of Ra, flipped horizontally. She considered herself "married" to Ra, but now I possessed a part of her.

A muted tapping sound made me lift my face toward the threshold of my room.

"Bastet?"

I sensed a warm presence.

She entered with a frown creasing her lips and her furry ears bent down with worry.

"What troubles you, my friend?" I asked, approaching

her and reaching out to touch her forearm. Her gaze shifted to avoid mine and she swallowed hard.

"You must be cautious, Horus," she replied. "Ra does not believe you are fulfilling your duties as he had intended."

"Why would he believe that?" I tilted my head. "He has not given me all my powers, but I have done with them what I can. I have limitations, still. What does he expect from me?"

"Horus, I..." She brought her face back up and looked me in the eye. I saw apprehension and fear in her palm-green irises. "I have witnessed your," her voice lowered to a whisper, "interactions with the head priestess of Ra. It is dangerous for you to be so involved with an acclaimed disciple."

"The mortal girl, Zahra?" I laughed heartily. "Why would Ra concern himself with a single human?"

"She may be mortal, but she is also *his*. You should not meddle in his affairs."

"Affairs?" I scowled. "The priestess was harmed last night, burned severely, and he did nothing to console her. He does not care about the loyalty of his worshippers, only the number of them. Did you see what he let happen to her? Did you see the terrible blisters upon her skin?"

It was brief and subtle, but I noticed a line of fur prickle on Bastet's forehead, just as her ears folded downward and then perked up again as her expression changed into an anxious grin.

She could not hide her body language from my attentive sight.

"Was that you?" I asked, narrowing my eyes. "Did *you* send feral cats through the alley so that they would cause the priestess to spill oil and catch fire? Why would you do such a horrid thing?" I took a step closer and used my fingers to tip Bastet's face up toward mine, forcing her wandering eyes to focus on me. I was tempted to be angry with her, but was also eager to hear her justification for the act; she was not one to make decisions in haste. "Why, Bastet?"

"I-I did not mean to harm her," she uttered, a look of shame making her ears go flat against her head. "I had only intended to frighten her—to expose her human frailty and cowardice to you and prove to you that she is not worthy of your guidance."

"You could have killed her!" I leaned in close. "And I would not have forgiven you for it."

"I only wish to protect you," she defended, sighing heavily. "You should not invest so much interest in one of Ra's coveted mortals."

"Although I appreciate your interest in my wellbeing, you have nothing to worry about," I replied. "The mortals know nothing of me. I am on a quest to regain my powers, as you had suggested, but how do I accomplish such a feat, and gain mortal faith, without revealing myself to them? I have found it difficult to cultivate trust from more than a few at a time since they cannot hear or see me."

Bastet crossed her arms and took a deep breath, lifting one hand to entwine her claws into her wesekh—the broad, colorful beaded golden collar around her neck. "There is a way," she muttered.

"A way to do what?"

She stood in silence, twisting a dangle of golden beads around her paw.

"Bastet?"

"To become visible to the humans," she said, looking away as if she had told me a dangerous secret. "To convey a human form."

"How?" My heart raced with excitement and the pounding in my chest made me tremble. "Tell me, please."

"There are other ways to gain the faith of the people," she whispered, changing the subject.

"No. You must tell me how to take a human form. That is what I wish to do, for I am certain I will gain followers if I can interact with them directly."

"There are many repercussions for doing so." Her worried eyes met mine. "Are you certain you want to do this?"

"Yes." I cupped one of her paws in my hands and squeezed gently. "I am strong and I do not fear the risks. I must do all I can to regain my powers. I must do all I can to prove myself to Ra and my uncle Set."

"Then there is something I must show you," she said, slipping her paw from my grasp. "Methods of acquiring followers have changed over the centuries; we do not use the same techniques we once did, because our presence is well established at this time." She swirled her paws in a circler motion and revealed an image of an emerald glass amphora capped with a polished copper plug. "Have you wondered how Ra acquired his human face?"

"Magic?" I had imagined his phenomenal power allowed him to simply create it, just as I had created my own disguise, but perhaps I was wrong.

"Yes," she confirmed, but then waved her paw across the image and drew the amphora much closer. "In order for us to take human form and become visible, we must choose a host whom we wish to inhabit." She stretched out a claw and pointed to the coil of faint light at the very bottom of the glass bottle. "But as long as we inhabit the host, their own ka remains imprisoned in an enchanted container such as this."

A withered ka lay crumpled on the glass floor, and it was then that I realized I had never seen Ra without his human façade.

"How long have they been imprisoned?" I peered at the desolate soul that was so ancient, most of its energy had faded.

"For as long as Ra has worn a human face."

A surge of resentment jolted through me and I clenched a fist. "So he stole the life of a mortal for his own selfish desires?"

"The Oath of the Gods forbids us from taking a life," Bastet corrected, dismissing the vision with a flick of her paw.

"So he trapped the human's ka for eternity? How does that differ from death?"

"I do not question the actions of our king. I have only showed you this in order to give you a way to interact with the mortals. Choose a host and use the time on Earth to spread word of the deeds of Horus and to gain disciples. Tell no one what I have told you."

"I understand," I replied with a nod. "Thank you for showing me this."

"I have left a vessel for you." She pointed toward a small blue clay jar in the corner of my room. "Use it wisely and with caution."

"Thank you. I will." I smiled at her. "Have faith in me, Bastet. How do you expect me to gain the people's faith, if I cannot gain that of a fellow friend and goddess?"

Her furry muzzle wrinkled as she grinned. "I *do* have faith in you, Horus. I always have." The words resonated with me, and I felt their truth granting me strength and confidence.

She tipped her head and then exited my room.

The thought of being able to be seen in the mortal realm excited me.

But, the thought of imprisoning a mortal's ka in order to do it... did not.

One soul was a small price to pay for a human face, but with Ra's supreme magic, I would have thought he could have done it the same way as I had—with imagination.

The cobalt sheen of the jar Bastet had left glistened, as if it were calling to me, longing to devour a soul, like the demon of the underworld. I approached it and wrapped my fingers around the piece, lifting it up from the floor. It had been made by a skilled craftsman, and its glaze fired to a flawless shine, exhibiting sparks of iridescent fire, which indicated it had been imbued with powerful magic.

Steal a mortal soul to gain mortal loyalty?

I grasped it firmly in my hand.

Even if I could release them once I had finished using their physical form, who was I to toy with the destiny of another? Who was I to take away hours, days, or even years from a mortal life?

I clenched a fist; the jar shattered in my hand and dissolved to dust.

I was not *Ra*...

10

ON THE outskirts of town, where no one would see, I planted my feet in the sand and raised my arms out in front of me, flexing my fingers anxiously.

Now that I had destroyed my chance at stealing a mortal body for the deed, I had to find a way to accomplish the feat of visibility without imprisoning one's ka.

I recalled the mighty stone statues guarding the entryway to Ra's temple, and an idea sparked to life. I gazed down at my golden sandals encrusted with precious jewels and visualized my body absorbing the earth through the soles of my feet. My fingers spun in a circular motion, making a swirl of sand drift toward me. Pale grains caressed my fingertips, reflecting sunlight as they danced across my skin.

Sand began to siphon up through my feet, filling each toe first, then rising toward my ankles and to my calves. It rose like the tide, fleshing out the curves of my thighs, the muscles of my abdomen and chest, and giving shape and solidity to that which was once transparent.

I swept my hands through the air, guiding each grain

into place until they had reached my neck and throat, and then my mouth, nose, and ears. The fair color allowed my hair to remain the light, wheat-like shade I had desired, but adversely faded my skin tone. To rectify that, I willed moisture from the air, pulling in enough to dampen and darken the sand to a more appropriate shade, while also sending the most saturated grains to my eyes, so that they would become a rich, amber hue.

Colors were missing still, so I bent down and pressed a flattened hand to the ground, calling upon limestone and basalt dusts to add texture and depth to my features. The whites and blacks lined my eyes and pupils, highlighted my hair, and gave contour to my muscles and joints.

I extracted flax fibers from the air, weaving them into a fine, short shendyt—the linen wrap covering me below the waist—and then I bent briefly again to pull flecks of gold from distant places deep below the surface, shaping them into carved armbands, a simple wesekh collar, and a narrow metallic belt. Though the reproduced features were not nearly as luxurious as my originals, they would have to do in the realm of the mortals. Only the richest mortals adorned themselves with opulent things, but if I sought to gain loyalties, I needed to stand out.

I turned my hands over and wiggled my fingers. They looked real enough, but something was off. My features were too pristine and statuesque—too much like chiseled stone.

Fusing the surface grains of sand together made them appear smoother and allowed me to convey a more natural skin-like texture, while keeping it flexible. I bent my arm and brought my hand in closer, raising it toward my face and spreading out my fingers. I rotated my wrist and turned my palm out to look over the bone structure and creases, making sure the sand had precisely filled in every detail.

Rays of sunlight twinkled off my hand, and I conjured another spell that muted the reflective properties of the glassy surface. Lastly, I forged a replica of my chest tattoo with coal and basalt because I would not hide my destiny from the people.

"Look at what I have done," I said, staring up into the sky. "What do you think?"

Something soft pressed against my ankle and I glanced down toward my feet. A small black cat was rubbing against my leg—one of Bastet's servants. I assumed it was a gesture of approval on the goddess' behalf. The cat flicked its tail and then scampered off.

The wind against my face felt more pronounced than it had before, and the wispy breeze on my cheeks was surprisingly pleasant. Once I arrived back in town, everything seemed new and different. Sounds were crisper and resonated more deeply through my ears. I brushed up against a vendor's stall table and the wood felt rough and dry to touch.

A man reached out toward me, his hand clutching a clump of wrinkled, brown balls which resembled animal dung.

"Have you tried my dates?" he shouted. He had to have known how close I was; there was no need to raise his voice.

I shook my head and pushed his arm from my way, continuing to shimmy through the bustling crowd. A quick glance around the place made me realize how poor the other townspeople were; people were plainly dressed in thick cotton and linen fabrics. Many eyes were already gawking at me because of my ornate jewelry, but I did not desire to draw quite *that much* attention to myself.

"You." I approached a stranger dressed in a white, hooded robe. "May I have your cloak?"

The man swiveled around and his eyes widened as he looked upon me. Then he let out a hearty laugh and glared. "*Give* you my cloak?" He threw his head back and chuckled. "What for? To cover that hideous hair of yours?" He gestured toward my head. "Your mother must have been forsaken by the gods."

Forsaken by the gods!?

I sneered.

My mother *was* a goddess.

His foolish comments provoked me, but I had to remain quiet and calm, so I bit my tongue and stared him straight in the eye.

"Hmm. You look well-off enough," he continued, shrugging. "Whoever you are. So what will you give me for it then?" He squinted one eye and raised his opposite brow into a high arch. His hand rose and he held out his palm.

I knelt on one knee and scooped up a handful of sand. I placed it in his hand and said, "Here." He instinctively closed his fingers tightly around the grains and a look of confusion twisted his face.

"Sand!? What do you take me for, you—" He unfurled his fingers and gasped at the brilliant blue gemstone glinting in his grasp. "Wh-what!?" He clasped the other hand over the jewel and swiftly tucked it away into a satchel hanging from his belt. The white robe slid off his back and he held it out to me. “It is yours,” he said, holding it up and helping to drape it over my shoulders.

“Thank you,” I replied, making slight adjustments to the way it fit and then flipping the hood over my head. I turned back toward him, but he had vanished.

“Odd man.”

At least now I could hide my “hideous” hair from the people, until I learned more about what I had to do to gain followers.

I craned my neck to look up at the sun, gazing into the ball of scorching light, past fire and magic, and through the window behind which Ra sat upon his throne. He was not looking back at me, and for that I was grateful.

Knowing he was not following my every move was a relief, and it reminded me that it was time to check on the priestess, Zahra, and see how she had recovered from the previous night’s mishap.

Past the crowded marketplace, a school room, and down several strangely less familiar alleyways—now that I could not sprint through them in ethereal form—stood the Temple of Ra.

Two other God’s Wives were out front, sweeping dirt from the main walkway and tossing flower petals down as they recited hymns. Nearby, little Nephiri, the youngest God’s Wife, knelt in the shade by a pillar, sketching on a papyrus sheet with a chip of charcoal pinched between her fingers.

“What are you drawing, young one?” I asked, leaning over to gaze down at her work. It was a malformed sketch of a bird-headed god, which could not possibly have been me. Perhaps it was Thoth, the ibis-headed god of knowledge and justice. But it did not resemble him, either.

"Who are you?" the child asked, looking up at me with a glint of fear in her eyes. "Strangers are not welcome here."

"I am a friend, Nephiri," I assured her with a smile. "You need not fear me." My fingers brushed across her bare shoulder and a glimmer of light kissed her skin, bestowing upon her a sense of calm.

"You know my name?" she asked, blinking curiously.

I had heard it before, while watching Zahra read to them at night.

"Yes." Changing the subject, I said, "So who is that you are drawing?" I pointed to the papyrus.

"Ra," she replied, but then narrowed her eyes at the drawing and huffed. "But I cannot draw him correctly."

"You know what he looks like?" I asked, pretending to be naïve. "Can you tell me?"

Nephiri tugged at my cloak so I would come down to her level, and I knelt to listen as she brought a hand to her mouth as if she were about to tell me a secret.

"He has the body of a man," she started quietly, "and the face of a beautiful falcon. He is strong and brave and kind. There is no other god more powerful than Ra."

I let out a chuckle of doubt and she gasped.

"How dare you laugh at Lord Ra!"

"My apologies," I replied. "I do not laugh at Ra. I only laugh because you believe there is no god who is more powerful."

She cocked her head to the side. "Is there?"

"Did you know that there is another falcon-headed god? His name is—" I remembered what Bastet had told me and hesitated. Then I opened my mouth to continue and—

"Get away from her!" Zahra roared.

I stood and turned to face the head priestess; her singed, ivory dress had been exchanged for a new one. She approached, and her brown eyes pierced mine, instilling a fleeting sensation of discomfort in me.

"I meant her no harm," I said, raising my empty hands as I backed away from the child.

"How dare you touch a God's Wife! You should leave!" Zahra's voice was even fiercer now. She looked me up and down quickly. "You have brought no offerings, so there is no place for you here."

"I wish to speak with you," I said.

She crossed her arms. "A priestess of Ra will hold no audience with a man."

"What is that?" I asked, pointing to the red cloth tied around her wrist, the one covering the mark I had given her the previous night.

"Th-this?" She instantly lost her brave composure. "It... it is nothing."

"Why would a priestess wear a scarlet band around her wrist?" I prodded. "Does it represent something? Was it a gift?"

"It..." She looked around frantically. "It was an injury."

"An injury, you say?" I repeated, working up a convincing look of great concern. "I hope you did not burn yourself. I know the priestesses must light many flames a night and... May I see it? My father was a healer and—"

"Come with me," Zahra interrupted. "Do not speak another word here." She pointed toward the entrance of the temple and ushered me inside. We stepped into the shadows and she motioned for me to follow her into a room off to the side that was lit brightly by candles and a small window in the wall that let in some of the sun's rays.

Zahra veered around and lifted her chin. "Remove your hood in this sacred place," she demanded, narrowing her eyes at me.

"Here? I..."

"You will show respect to our Lord Ra or I will dismiss you at once."

I did not feel comfortable revealing myself to her yet, so I changed the subject as quickly as I could and said, "What do you hide there on your wrist? God's Wives are supposed to be pure, are they not?"

Her jaw dropped and she sucked in a breath. Her heart began to race and she tangled her fingers together.

"I am hiding nothing," she replied quickly, though the fearful look in her eyes contradicted her words.

"I thought God's Wives were to only speak truth," I said, stepping closer to her.

She looked around to make sure no other wives were in the room and then shakily asked, "Who are you? Why do you accuse me of such things?"

"I..." I was so close to revealing to her the truth. My name was at the tip of my tongue, but I did not want to break the Oath of the Gods. "I cannot tell you just yet," was all I could reply. "I am sorry, but I must go." I turned away from her, but just as I did, she darted forward, reached up, clasped the back of my hood, and pulled it down off my head.

A soft, frightened yelp escaped her mouth. "What are you?" she asked, her voice trembling. "Y-your hair is as fair as sand."

I turned my head to the side. "I am human. Why would you ask a question like that?"

"Then where are you from?"

The temptation to speak the truth overwhelmed me and I raised a hand and pointed toward the ceiling. "Far away," I replied.

"What does that mean?" she retorted, coming around to face me head on again. "Are you from another city? If so, which one? I am not an ignorant woman. Do not lie to me, please."

"You are the only one here who tells a lie, Zahra," I said, flicking a hand toward her; the red cloth tore from her wrist and fell to the ground.

She covered her mark with her other hand. "How dare you!" she cried, shaking with anger and embarrassment. "I demand you leave this temple now."

I shook my head. Seeing her in distress was uncomfortable, and I felt inclined to retreat and let her be, but I could not ignore why I had come to her again.

"I know what it means," I said, pointing to her wrist.

"I asked you to leave," she spoke through gritted teeth, pointing toward the entryway.

"Why are you afraid to tell me about the mark? Are you ashamed of it?"

Zahra lowered her head and her jaw tightened. "No. I am not ashamed of a gift from a god." Her eyes met mine and a fierce spark of determination burned in them. "They protected me in a time of need, and now I bear this symbol as a reminder of the debt I owe."

"You owe me nothing but loyalty," I said.

"Owe *you!?*" She huffed and unclasped her hands to point a stiff finger at me. "You spew vanity and arrogance. The gods will punish you for your insolence. I am a God's Wife, and you cannot harass me like this."

"You are a God's Wife, Zahra," I spoke softly, taking another step closer, though she recoiled. "And I am a god."

Her eyes widened. "How dare you!? As head priestess, I demand respect!"

"And I demand gratitude!"

She bolted at me and raised her hand to strike, but, like a viper, I caught her by the wrist. My fingers squeezed firmly, but gently, and the magic in my veins began to churn, pushing me to show her the truth, even as my heart knew that it would mean breaking the Oath.

"I do not lie," I whispered, lowering my face toward hers as she continued to bare her teeth and growl like a cornered animal. She could not intimidate me, but her strength made me proud to have chosen her as a disciple.

She wriggled and tried to pull away, but I held fast. "Do you wish to know me better?" I asked, allowing a splash of dark brown and white feathers to flash across my face.

Zahra screeched and I released her; she lost her footing and stumbled to the floor.

"Two cats rushed by the other night," I started, kneeling before her. "They caused you to trip and spill lamp oil upon your dress."

Zahra started to shake and a muffled whimper escaped

her mouth.

"Your leg was badly burned and you suffered blisters and swelling on your ankle and calf."

She shook her head in disbelief. "H-how do you know that?"

I stood. "That mark is the eye of Horus, God of the Sky."

Bewildered, she silently mouthed my name.

"I am Horus," I continued, shedding the cloak I had acquired, forcing it to disperse into individual threads which remained suspended in the air around me. My jewelry twinkled as thin rays of sunlight peeked in through the window and danced across the gold's surface. Then I willed sand to diffuse from my body and cast the shape and patterns of a falcon's face over mine, the particles glittering like gemstones as they revealed my true form to the priestess.

She sat there in awe, her hands cupped over her mouth, presumably to muffle the scream welling in her throat.

"Do not fear me, Zahra." I bent down; she yelped and cowered, looking away. "Zahra?"

"Forgive me," she whimpered, bowing low to the ground. Her breaths were short and her heartbeat pulsed like a drum.

"You may look upon me," I said.

She grunted softly as she came to her knees and then stood and straightened up, still avoiding my face. She swept her hands over her skirt and swallowed hard.

"Zahra?" I dismissed my falcon façade.

Finally, she lifted her gaze and looked at me. Her head tilted. "That tattoo," she said, pointing at my chest, "is similar in design to..." Her hand came up and she turned her wrist over.

The large tattoo on my chest was below my collar bone and spread part-way across my pectorals; I had been born with it. The center was an intricate eye, a variation of Ra's facing the opposite direction. The left side featured the vulture goddess, Nekhbet, with wings spread, wearing the white crown of Upper Egypt. The right side was a depiction of the cobra goddess, Wadjet, with the red crown of Lower Egypt upon her head.

"Were you sent by Ra to defend me?" Zahra asked.

"Ra has sent no one to your aid," I replied with a muted scoff. "I have chosen to look after you of my own accord."

"You... *chose* me? Why? I am but a lowly priestess, and—"

"You are loyal," I interjected, lifting a hand to her cheek. She flinched, at first, but then froze as I stroked the back of my fingers across her skin, leaving a trace of magic dust upon her face. "Dedicated to your beliefs."

"Yes... but... I..." The words trickled from her lips as if she could not find them quickly enough. "I..."

My fingers slipped beneath her face and I tipped her chin up. The brilliant blue-green eyeshadow sparkled above her rich, brown eyes, and her crimson lip stain seemed more apparent than before. Behind the makeup, though, her eyes were still delicate and fine and her features quite pleasant.

"What is it?" Zahra asked, squinting. "Why do you search my soul? What is it you seek, Lord Horus?"

I suddenly did not know...

What did I seek?

I was sure I once sought power and the magic to grow and to prove myself to Ra and Uncle Set, but as Zahra's dark eyes searched mine, those desires drifted away and new ones filtered in. Desires I had not felt before, nor that I understood how to interpret.

I had longed to convert the head priestess of Ra into a follower so that her prominence might grant me greater magic and her influence might sway the faiths of the people of Egypt.

But now, I could not focus on that end.

I wanted a new companion—one who could never be forced from my side; one who could support me in times of strife.

Although Bastet had been my companion and confidant for many centuries, her friendship endangered us both. Ra could take it away from me at any moment, forcing my dear friend to forsake her stature for favoring another god above her king.

"Tell no one of this encounter," I said flatly, my hand sliding from her face.

She nodded.

"Leave the lamps burning at night; I will take away the flames when I return. I will come when Ra rests and Nut shares the sky with her children. Expect me then."

"Yes, Lord Horus," she replied.

Then I remembered the brand I had placed upon her wrist and thought of her safety. I used a spark of magic to bring her scarlet cloth up off the floor, shake off the sand, and then loop it around her wrist again, tying the ends together gently.

Her once distressed and angry expression had changed to one of curiosity, and she now looked at me with a sense of warmth and intrigue. Her pulse had softened and her sharp tongue quieted, and for both I was thankful.

"I will return," I said, and in the blink of her eyes, I vanished into a mist of sand and earth.

11

MORNING came and went and few duties remained in my afternoon. I altered the tides and upset the stillness of the lakes by dragging wind across them until they rippled like linen in the breeze. Then I shifted the direction of the wind currents to assist the birds and guide them safely home to their nests before evening approached.

All the while, I fought to sort out new, unsettling thoughts twisting through me. How had Zahra occupied so much of my mind that I had momentarily lost sight of my intentions in the mortal realm?

I *required* loyal followers, and she had proven herself to be one of the most dedicated servants of Ra. Surely I had not broken the Oath of the Gods by favoring the priestess above other mortals.

My powers were all that mattered.

But still, I pondered how it was possible for gods to be forbidden from showing compassion and dedication toward each other, but expected and demanded such from the mortals, in return for very little.

Bastet's friendship had to be kept secret from our king, or he could banish her for showing favoritism to me. But my mother could devote herself to the mothers and daughters of the entire land and never be questioned, even as her own son was often abandoned and neglected.

The Oath did not always make sense; we were not to question it.

Light began to fade from the sky and I glanced up to see Ra escorting the sun across the horizon with his flaming chariot pulled by golden stallions. Nut and her children would soon gain control of the night, and darkness would fall upon the land.

In the distance, through stone and wood, man and beast, I saw Zahra lighting oil lamps around the perimeter of the temple. As head priestess, she had done this each night at dusk in a ceremonial effort. God's Wives believe the ritual guides Ra home to his temple after dark. After the moon had risen, she would extinguish the flames so that he could rest and recover there.

I watched her as I had the night before, looming in distant shadows for some time as I juggled anxious ideas and desires. After all the other wives had gone to sleep, and while Zahra sat upon the edge of her cot, struggling to discipline herself enough to leave the lamps burning long past their usual time, I decided to visit her again.

I flicked my hand, dismissed the flames dancing outside the temple, and then passed through the walls and entered her bed chamber, remaining invisible. She sat hunched over on her bed, gazing down at the cloth tied around her wrist.

I approached her slowly and tugged at the knot to get

her attention. She shifted and looked up.

"Are you there?" she asked.

I willed sand and elements to me once more, and she watched, entranced, as I materialized before her.

"Thank you for returning, Lord Horus," she said, standing to greet me.

I put out a flattened hand and stopped her. "Stay seated, please." She paused and then sat back down.

"I apologize for my untidiness," she said, looking at her bedcover and attempting to smooth it out with several strokes of her hands.

"Do not worry yourself with such petty things," I assured her and then took a seat beside her. Her pupils grew dark as she eagerly awaited my next words.

I separated my lips to speak, but...

Words did not come.

A moment had passed until I realized my thoughts had fallen upon her face and that my attention had been ensnared by her rich brown eyes.

Her long, glossy black hair shimmered like polished onyx beneath the candlelight, shifting with her as she tipped her head and stared back at me with a look of confusion upon her face.

"I am a god, and you are a God's Wife," I finally got out, "and yet I cannot put into words my thoughts, for I do not comprehend them myself."

"I am sorry, but I do not understand what you mean," she replied.

"I am the *Sky* God, and my duties lie *there*," I pointed up, "yet when I am *there*, my mind remains here with you."

Her eyes widened and she gasped.

"So you *do* understand?" I asked. A shimmer of candlelight glistened off her eyes and tears threatened to fall upon her cheeks. I lifted a hand to cup her face. "Zahra, what is it?"

"He will punish me if I betray him," she murmured.

"Who?"

"Lord Ra. You cannot come to me and say such things. It dishonors my sworn oath to be his wife."

"You believe Ra will pass judgment upon you for speaking to me?"

"You have touched me twice already."

And I *would* touch her again...

"Ra did not come to your aid when you needed him. He did not extinguish the flames that endangered you, and he did not soothe the violent heat blistering your leg."

Zahra's lip trembled.

"You are a God's Wife," I said, reaching out to touch her face again. "Does it matter which god?"

"I am sworn to Ra!" She jerked back. "I will not betray my lord."

"If Ra does not come for you, then there is no one to betray." I reached up a hand to press my fingers to her bare shoulder and grasp the strap of her dress. "He did not protect you then, either." I gestured toward the scar on her back and the intensity of her expression softened.

"Y-you are right," she murmured, bringing her arms up to embrace herself tightly. "Ra did not protect me when I was a child, and he did not protect me the night of the fire. Doubts had risen in my heart before, but I had cursed myself for questioning my faith. Forgive me. I am a fool to question a god who stands before me—a god who *has* shown me compassion."

Her change of heart sent a whirlwind of fresh magic through me, warming my body with a surge of bright new power and purpose. The exhilarating jolt excited me and a rush of desire consumed my thoughts. I took hold of Zahra's shoulders, leaned closer until our noses nearly touched, looked into her eyes, and then whispered, "Become mine."

A sharp breath sounded from her.

She silently echoed my words.

I searched her anxious irises for the answer, but I could not read her.

"Give me your answer now," I commanded, and instantly sensed her reply—my amulet began to hum softly and it grew hot against my skin. The warmth infiltrated every vein and every particle of my flesh, enveloping me in potent magic. I glanced down at it and witnessed one of the deeper cracks drawing closed as it healed.

Zahra's faith alone had provided me with a burst of power stronger than a hundred common mortals.

"Well?" I asked again, loosening my grasp on her arms and getting up from her bed. "Will you accept *me* as your god?"

I needed to hear the words.

She looked up into my eyes and opened her mouth to speak, but nothing came out.

My gaze remained locked onto hers as I waited.

She slowly nodded.

An uncontrollable smile coiled my lips as her newfound

faith sent a wave of visceral heat over me.

She had called it "betrayal," at first, but our bond would benefit us both.

Zahra would gain protection and I would gain strength.

Together, we would sway the people of Egypt, and I would show Ra how capable I really was, by fulfilling my destiny without his help.

"You have made a wise choice, Zahra," I spoke. "You will never have to worry about facing such terrible things again, because you will be under my protection."

"Thank you," she replied, her voice breaking.

"That scar—I will make it go away." I lifted my fingers toward her shoulder, but she recoiled.

"No."

"No?" I paused, my hand lingering a few inches from her skin. "As a God's Wife, you should not carry a haunting mark upon your perfect skin. I wish to rid you of it."

"Please allow me to keep it," she muttered, afraid to make eye contact with me.

"Why? What reason do you have to retain it?"

"My scar reminds me of my past," she started shakily. "And... it will serve as... as a reminder of Ra's abandonment."

There was defeat in her voice, and the sadness in her eyes had me momentarily rethinking my desire to make her mine.

"Then you may keep it," I replied, shoving the disconcerting thoughts from my mind. Ra did not need her in his flock, and he would not notice one missing sheep.

I looked down at Zahra and asked, "Would you walk with me?"

She seemed surprised by my request, but quickly pushed up from her bed and bowed. "Yes, my lord."

My lord?

I could not decide if I liked the sound of that or not. She was my servant, but I was not her king.

Not yet.

"Where do you wish to go?" she asked, stepping beside me and tangling her hands together.

"To see a friend." I began to walk toward the temple's main entrance, but as I did, she did not follow. I turned to face her again. "What is wrong?"

"I... cannot be seen with a man."

"I am a god."

"Yes, my lord, you are a god," she corrected herself, "but the people of my village do not know this, nor will they see you as such in the form you take now. It could cause a great uproar, should such an accusation be made of me."

"You are under my protection."

She chewed her lip and swallowed hard.

I did not like the sense of worry exuding from her.

Perhaps there was another way.

I did not have all my powers, but Bastet had told me that the temples of the gods were great sources of magic, even if they were not dedicated to me.

"Zahra?"

"Yes?"

"Come to me."

She hesitantly inched closer.

I reached out and brought her in near to my chest. She began to quake with fear and her breaths hastened. Her heartbeat thumped through me as I embraced her tightly.

Next, I tried to visualize the magic of the temple and all its followers as if it were light surrounding our bodies. To cast a spell properly, all one had to do was picture clearly in the mind's eye exactly the outcome one intends. For me, that outcome was to make transportation from this temple to another possible.

She began to shudder, and I tightened my hold on her in an effort to calm her fears, but she shook even more, my touch pushing her over the edge of her comfort zone.

"Do not fear me, Zahra," I whispered, pressing her body to mine. "Do not fear my power."

Golden light began to saturate the room and her anxious pulse began to slow. A swirl of white fire engulfed us and Zahra suddenly raised her hands to cling to me tightly.

Everything turned white.

The light faded and blackness surrounded us.

A flick of my hand lit a row of candles that had already been in the room, casting a warm glow upon the basalt statue of Bastet standing tall before us.

Zahra released me and I her.

"The temple of Bastet," she whispered, looking around. "Why are we here?"

"Bastet is my greatest ally in the Palace of the Gods. I have brought you here so that she may meet you formally, and so that she might extend to you her protection, as well, in return for your loyalty toward me."

"What of your mother? Does she not care for you?"

"Isis has not watched over me since I was a child. She busies herself with the prayers of mortal women and children."

"I am sorry to know that," Zahra said, looking up at me with a glint of sympathy in her eyes. "I hope she will not judge me cruelly for the way I had shunned my nephew, but—"

"She will not," I assured her. "My mother is forgiving."

Zahra looked up at the statue of Bastet, which held a long golden staff and stood in a rigid pose. "Bastet is a benevolent goddess, and word of her miracles has spread far and wide," she said, tilting her head. "You must have done great things to have earned her companionship."

I approached the statue and reached out to brush my fingers against an ankh that was clasped in the statue's other hand.

"Bastet is a ferocious warrior who carries with her the vitality and bravery of a thousand lions. Her power is dwarfed only by the great amount of compassion within her heart."

One of the walls of the room had a carving of the Feather of Truth accented with gold and surrounded by etchings of small cats. I pointed to it and said, "When weighed against the Feather of Truth, Bastet's heart did not tip the scale even the slightest, for she is composed of purity and righteousness."

Zahra smiled up at the statue.

"Are you feeling all right?" I asked, noticing that her eyelids appeared heavy.

"I am sorry, but I grow tired."

I had forgotten about the necessity of mortal sleep.

"I understand," I replied. "I will return you to your temple. Come." I motioned for her to approach me again. As she shuffled closer and I opened my arms to receive her, the floor began to quake.

I lost my footing, the room went black, and I tumbled into darkness.

As I stood and shook my head, I could make out Zahra's silhouette in the distance. She was frozen in time and encased in flickering spires of blue light.

"Zahra!" I moved toward her but made no progress as the earth seemed to move against me, making each step futile.

The statue of Bastet reappeared, its eyes aglow with molten orange. Dense fog wafted from the floor and my head felt heavy.

"What do you think you are doing!?" a powerful voice roared, piercing my ears like a bell.

The statue's mouth opened. "What is this insolence, Horus!?" it growled.

Had she stopped time? I had not realized a god could be capable of such a feat.

"Let Zahra go," I commanded.

The statue's head cocked. "Why do you insist on defying our king? Ra will not let such defiance go without punishment."

Bastet raised her staff and pointed to the distance. Her face shifted and her expression bent into a deep frown. "Your association with the priestess goes against the Oath," she added in a softer voice. "You must not favor another! And of all people, you have seized the head priestess and wife of Ra."

"I am no longer a child, Bastet," I replied. "Leave me to my judgment, be it wrong or right in your eyes."

"Listen, Horus, for I risk much in coming to you now. I, too, have broken the Oath by insisting upon secretly retaining our friendship, even as Ra has questioned me about it. I have also kept your activities here on Earth private from our king, even while doing so could—"

"If I require your counsel, I will ask for it. Now free Zahra immediately, and send me back to the mortal realm."

The statue's eyes faded to a soft golden hue and she lowered her staff. "Please heed my warnings, Horus, as a friend," she said. "You do not have the power to challenge Ra."

"Not yet," I muttered, clenching my fists, "but I will."

Bastet's head fell and she sighed, defeated. "I have warned you. I will not be able to come to your aid, should Ra find out about this."

"I understand, and I will not hold a grudge against you." I pressed a fist to my chest briefly and tipped my head toward her. "Now free the priestess and leave me be."

The fog faded, the blue light vanished from Zahra, and the walls of the temple reappeared, illuminated by warm candle flames.

Zahra pressed close to my chest and embraced me. I wrapped my arms around her and we were again consumed by white light.

My feet landed on sand and stone and we were back in Zahra's chamber inside the Temple of Ra. She released me and stepped back.

"I will pray to your friend, Bastet," she said, a small smile curling her lips. "So that she will know how grateful I am for her and your protection."

Bastet's warning resonated in my mind.

"My lord?" Zahra's fingers brushed against my arm. "Is something wrong?"

I glanced down into her worried eyes.

"No," I lied. She did not need to know about Bastet's intervention.

Zahra's growing faith in me had granted me new magic, making me stronger. How could something so pure, so empowering, be considered disgraceful?

Bastet obviously felt compassion toward me, and my mother, Isis, had coveted my father, Osiris, for centuries. Yet somehow, my trivial pursuit of a single God's Wife was appalling and forbidden?

All nonsense, spread to stop me from acquiring my true abilities.

"You may sleep now," I whispered to Zahra. Her fingers slipped from my arm and the warmth of her touch dissipated from my skin. "I will watch over you."

12

Despite Bastet's warning, I continued visiting Zahra. I was vigilant in carrying out my duties during the day and went only after dark, so that my absence would go unnoticed in the Palace of the Gods.

Each moment spent in her company cultivated my magic. I listened to her tell stories about the gods to the other wives in the evenings, after which I would take her aside and gently correct her details so that she could amend them in her tomes.

In the days that passed, I temporarily disregarded my desire to gain the worship of all people and concentrated on garnering Zahra's complete trust and devotion. Her companionship provided me with a sense of wholeness and belonging that I had not experienced in the Palace of the Gods; each healed fracture of my amulet encouraged me to continue on my current path. Once my stone fully healed, I planned on working with Zahra to pursue the worship of the other followers of Ra, and then use those influences to ensnare the remaining villagers and—ultimately—the acting Pharaoh.

The sun set and I soared across the sky, over other gods'

temples, and toward the faint lamplight flickering around the perimeter of Ra's—the guiding flames Zahra left burning for me each night.

I drifted past the entryway, through the walls dividing the rooms, and then swooped down into Zahra's chamber. She sat upon her bed, her knees pulled to her chest and her head buried in her folded arms. Her breaths were inconsistent and her heartbeat thumped fervently.

As I manifested before her of sand, stone, and gold, she did not raise her head to greet me. "Zahra?" I spoke softly as I approached and stretched out an arm to touch her. She winced and let out a frightened yelp. "What has happened?" I asked, looking her over swiftly; I could not see anything out of place. "You must speak to me, Zahra."

Finally, she raised her head just enough for me to spot a dash of blood trailing down her cheek. The sight of crimson on her face ignited the fire of rage inside me. I reached for her arm, forcing her to uncover her face completely.

"What happened?" I squeezed her arm harder than I had intended. She flinched and grunted, and I quickly released her.

"I-I..." She heaved short breaths.

I knelt on the edge of her bed, lifted her face toward me, and gently caressed my fingers over the wound. It was deep, but clean—clearly made by a blade. Zahra trembled, tears continuing to stream as I turned her face from one side to the other to check for additional wounds. Although I did not see any more blood, dark purple bruises marred her throat and forearms—one of which was the distinct imprint of a hand that had clutched her roughly.

Whatever it was that had happened, I despised myself for not having been there to stop it.

I pressed a hand against her bloody wound and cast a healing spell upon it. She shuddered, but then glanced up into my eyes and opened her mouth to speak.

"M-my lord..." was all she could stammer. She swiped her palms across her eyes to try to dry the tears.

"Who did this to you!?" My voice became gruff and I clasped onto her tightly, unwittingly pressing my fingers against her bruises.

She cried out and I released her again.

"Forgive me, Zahra!" I stroked a hand through her hair and concentrated on forcing more magic to the surface of my fingertips. The warm light sunk into her skin and caused the unsightly colored blotches to fade away. "You must tell me exactly what happened."

"I went to the market with Nephiri," she started slowly, clutching her wrist in close to her chest. "My cloth caught on something and was torn away." She gazed up at me with large, frightened eyes and shuddered again. "I tried to cover it quickly, but... someone saw the mark and..."

"They dared to harm you for it!?" I forced myself up from her bed and gritted my teeth.

"They claimed to be followers of Ra and interpreted the image as a means of disloyalty. They marked my face so that others would know of my deceit, and..." She started crying again. "Please, take it back." She held out her hand.

"I will not," I replied firmly, shaking my head. "How are you so eager to return such a gift, while you begged me to allow you to harbor the scar of Ra's negligence? I *promised* to protect you—"

"You can take away bruises and scars, but you cannot erase my memories," she replied. "I have suffered for my faith before, and it continues, even as I naïvely believed it would end after you appeared." Zahra's lip trembled and she sucked in sharp, labored breaths, hunching over to hold herself and look away from me. "I want peace."

How had I failed to keep her safe?

What if it had been worse?

What if the beasts had taken her life?

"I will not remove the mark," I said to her. "You are mine now, and I *will* avenge the attack made upon you."

Her face began to rise again and just as her teary eyes looked back at me, I dispersed into my invisible form and whisked out of the temple in a flurry of glimmering sand.

I bolted through the streets at the speed of an arrow, searching for the mortal who had harmed Zahra. From the handprints on her neck and arm, I could gather enough information to pick him out of a crowd, but as I soared through the dark pathways, there were no crowds to even consider.

The marketplace was deserted, but a faint glow drew my attention. In the distance, on a plank of wood that made up part of a vendor's stall, was a faded smudge of red—Zahra's blood—glimmering in the moonlight.

I stopped in front of it and brushed my fingers across the rust-colored stain. A flash of the culprit rattled my brain—a husky man with a thick, dirty beard—braided into two parts—and a wide silver collar of chains around his neck. On his forehead was a deep-set scar in the shape of a crudely drawn *was scepter*, a loose interpretation of the staff carried by my uncle, Set. It was associated with domination, power... *and chaos.*

Visions collided in my mind—images of the assailant slicing a dagger down her face and watching her bleed, of her hands bound by rope, and her shoulders held tightly by another whose face I could not define. Like flint against stone, a violent flash showed the leader striking her across the face.

I hissed and clenched my hands into fists. A second glance at the bloody mark on the wood summoned an apparition to appear—a phantom of the past, an account of where the villains had taken Zahra before she had escaped.

I pursued them faster than a storm, their transparent shapes guiding me through sand and stone passageways, each twist and turn bringing me closer and closer to finding their lair.

The apparitions led me to a cellar tucked away behind a small inn. I shot through the entryway, leaving the wooden doors swinging open and clacking against the wind.

They were there inside the hidden storehouse; the past could not lie.

My abrupt entrance left them stunned and wary and the men jolted up from their seats. There were two men in my vision, but three stood before me: the aggressor, his accomplice, and a witness.

The assailant drew a dagger from a shaft on his belt and crept toward the doors in an offensive stance, while the accomplice lagged behind and gawked over his shoulder. The witness sat in the far corner, seemingly inattentive while whittling a shape from a piece of wood.

"Who is there?" the bearded man with the thick metal

collar asked, poking his head out the entrance. It was pitch black outside. He looked both ways and then let out a disgruntled huff, tucking his dagger away. He grabbed hold of the doors and pulled them closed, fastening them shut by slipping a metal hook between a pair of rings affixed to the insides of each.

"What was that?" the accomplice asked, scratching his neck.

"The wind," the assailant replied with a gruff snarl. I assumed he was the leader of the three, as he was the biggest, and exhibited such behavior and commanding traits. It was indeed the man I had been searching for; the indentation of the *was scepter* disfigured his forehead and distinct chains jingled from his neck.

A glow resonated from his sleeves—remnants of Zahra's blood. The sight of the crimson light emanating from the fabric of his shirt enraged me, and I willed the sand and elements to make me visible again. The commotion jarred all three men to attention and they drew weapons, facing the swirl of magic and earth emerging in the center of the small, dank storehouse.

"What you have done is unforgivable," I boomed, my body only half manifested. My fingers tingled and burned with fierce energy. Revenge magnified the light inside me, feeding the fire of rage with sparks of wild magic. Sand fused together, solidifying my skin while particles of gold and jewels curled around my arms and neck, forming my amulet and arm bands.

"Who are you?" the leader asked, glaring while pointing his dagger in my direction. A hint of Zahra's blood still colored the blade.

"Why did you harm the God's Wife?" I spoke, baring my teeth. "Who sent you to commit such an atrocity?"

The leader's pulse rose and his heart thumped in his chest; he could not stop shaking.

"She committed treason with that mark on her wrist," he replied. "She needed to be punished."

"And you think it is your responsibility to punish traitors?" I approached him and narrowed my eyes. "Why not leave it to the gods to pass judgment?"

"Our god leaves that to us." He pointed a rigid thumb at his chest. "We would have put an end to her, had she not gotten away, but I will pass that judgment on to you, since you seem so eager for it."

The man lunged forward, jabbing his dagger into my chest. The metal wedged into the fused sand and he could not pull it free. I absorbed the last trace of Zahra's blood from the metal, and then forced the grains of sand to shift just enough to flip the knife around until it faced its master. The jagged metal protruded toward him from my sternum.

"You cannot harm a god with a man-made dagger," I growled. "How dare you even try!"

The leader stumbled backward a few steps. "What are you!?"

"Ask Lord Anubis," I replied, "before he feeds your iron hearts to the demon beast, Ammit."

Once Ammit devoured a heart, there was no chance for peace or rebirth... These men deserved neither.

While the third man remained still, the accomplice came at me with a scythe, charging toward my stomach. He reeled back and came down hard, wedging the blade into my waist and losing his footing as the strike sent a jarring vibration through his bones. I pulled the weapon from me, waited for the crack to seal and the grains to come back together, and then held the blade out toward them.

"Our god will make you pay for threatening us!" the leader howled. He unraveled a thick linen scarf from around his throat and revealed a dark tattoo crudely scribbled at the base of his neck. I recognized the mark immediately—the figure with stubby, mutilated ears, an exaggerated long face, and the staff of chaos grasped firmly in his boney fingers.

Set.

These men were not followers of Ra, they were followers of Set! The scar on his forehead had been an indication, but the tattoo verified it.

I swept my arms up, pulled every fleck of sand from the floor into the air, and then forced it at the men, thrusting them against the stone wall at the back of the room. They let out loud gasps as the wind was knocked from their lungs and the abrasive sand crashed into their eyes and mouths.

They fell, hitting the ground with thuds. Howls of pain curdled in their throats and they writhed about on the floor, spitting and shaking their heads violently.

"Do you want a chance at rebirth?" I asked, stepping closer to the mound of sand and stone they lay flailing in. "Renounce your loyalty to Set. Accept me, Horus, God of the Sky, as your lord, and I will relieve you of your moral debts."

All three remained quiet and continued to shake and groan.

"What say you?" I concentrated on the scar on the leader's forehead and traced the design with invisible fire, making him clutch his face in pain. There had to be a way to break him.

Then a hand lifted and the accomplice raised his head and blinked rapidly. "I-I will," he croaked weakly, squinting as debris still blinded him.

The leader let out an angry roar and pushed up from the ground, bolting toward the other man and shoving him facedown back into the sand. The accomplice struggled beneath his leader, but the larger man easily overpowered him and kept him pinned and unable to breathe. He reached for his scarf with one outstretched arm and roped it around the man's neck.

"Stop!" I yelled, but the leader continued strangling the other man. The horrible gagging sounds made my heart race.

In a panic, I thrust my arms out, sending a wall of light, earth, and metal flying into the air.

The entire room fell silent.

Everything settled.

An even larger mound of earth had piled up against the wall.

I dropped the scythe and flicked my hands, brushing away the top layer to uncover the three men.

The man who had chosen not to attack me rolled over onto his back and coughed hard, in pain, but alive.

The accomplice lay silent and still, the wind of life already pulled from his lungs before I could stop it.

And the leader lay flat on his belly, a pool of red

saturating the sand around him. I used my powers to flip him onto his back and saw that the dagger I had pulled from him—the one which he had used to harm Zahra—had been forced straight through his chest, killing him instantly.

We were not to kill...

It said so in the Oath of the Gods. But...

It was an accident and...

"You!" I pointed at the remaining thug, straining to hide the rising fear rattling my voice. "Do you submit to me? Will you accept me as your god and denounce Set!?"

A glimmer of warm yellow light sparkled at my fingertips as the man nodded and shuddered.

"Good." I approached him and bent over to look him in the eye. "Tell others of the punishments for angering the Sky God, Horus, and what they will face when harming my servants, and remember that a benevolent god has spared your life this day." I flashed an image of my falcon face, my feathers perked up, and I opened my beak to let out a terrible screech. The man's eyes widened and then his irises rolled back into his head and he fainted.

I took wing to the evening breeze and soared back to the Temple of Ra. There, I found Zahra on the edge of her bed in her room, cradling little Nephiri in an embrace.

I did not manifest immediately, but instead hovered nearby and whispered so that only she could hear, "We must speak."

Zahra looked up and nodded in acknowledgement.

"Nephiri?" She forked her fingers through the little one's hair and smiled down at her. "You must go to bed now.

Things will be different in the morning."

Nephiri was hesitant to leave, at first. I reached down to press a finger to her shoulder, infusing her with a hint of calming magic, and then she finally slid off Zahra's bed and left.

I became visible and approached Zahra slowly.

"Is Nephiri going to be all right?" I asked.

She nodded. "I believe so. She hid when I was captured and, although it was traumatizing for her to witness, the fact that I am healed now has lessened some of her anxiety. She has not spoken a word since the incident, however."

"I believe she will be fine." I sat beside her on the bed. A sudden heaviness overwhelmed me and I lowered my head. "I am sorry I was not there to help you when you needed me. I promised to keep you safe and I failed."

"What if they are not the last to challenge my faith? What if more come for me? I am frightened, and I must keep the other wives safe, too."

"Those men *will* be the last to harm you," I said.

"They will? But—"

I turned to her and looked straight into her teary eyes, a deep, unusual sensation of sickness twisting my stomach.

She gasped. "What have you done!?"

I could not find the strength to open my mouth and tell her the truth, for it made me feel ashamed. I had not meant to kill. I did not know what my intentions were, but they were not to kill.

"I have done all this only for you, Zahra," I whispered. "My responsibilities as God of the Sky have fallen second only to your company... and when that became threatened,

I—"

She lifted her arms up, and her gentle hands wrapped around to my back. I lowered my head to her shoulder and let her pull me into an embrace.

"I understand," she spoke, her voice as calm as still water. "There is no need to worry now." Her delicate fingers brushed through the back of my hair and her soft breaths soothed my tense muscles. "Thank you for returning to me."

I had never understood the mortal sensation of pain, but suddenly, my heart began to ache.

13

DID ZAHRA understand what I had done?

Did she know someone had died by my hand?

She held me close, and while her tight embrace was meant to console me, the rapid fluttering of her heart conveyed how frightened she really was.

I did not know how to settle her fears.

Or my own.

The vast, open sky and whispers of the night could soothe my racing mind, but could the subtle melodies of languid beasts and slumbering earth offer her the same solace as it did me?

It was worth a try.

"Would you walk with me?" I asked, lifting my head off her shoulder so that I could look into her mink-brown eyes.

Zahra cocked her head and looked as if she might speak, but nothing came out of her parted lips. She feared leaving the temple after dark, and of being seen with a man. But I could—I *would*—protect her from anything that dared to stalk her from the shadows.

I took the initiative, stood, and offered her my hand. Again, she gazed at me and said nothing.

"Please?" I asked, bending and offering out my hand even farther. "Do not fear being seen beside me, and do not think of me as a mortal man, for I am anything but."

She lifted her arm as if she might lay her fingers on mine, but then withdrew. Then she stood and nodded, forcing a smile. "Yes. Let us walk together. Shall I bring a lamp?"

"No. *I* will guide you."

After the other God's Wives had gone to sleep, Zahra and I left the temple and wandered into the night. As shadows fell upon me, I loosened my control over the sands that formed my flesh, allowing the grains to separate only enough that a faint warm aura could shine through.

Zahra gasped as the glow washed over me; it started at my feet and then climbed toward my head, until every inch of my skin emanated faint magical radiance. With no witnesses in sight, I began guiding her through the village streets.

We walked for quite some time before nearing the outskirts of the city. From there, I saw distant sparkles of moonlight dancing across ripples of the River Nile.

"Where are we going?" Zahra asked, following beside me and barely brushing against my arm with each step we took in tandem.

"To the river," I replied, looking over at her. "My," the urge to say 'battle' tempted me, but I repressed it and continued, "encounter earlier required a great amount of strength, and my magic has been drained significantly. I do not tire as you mortals do, but a sensation of minor weakness beseeches me to rest." I pointed ahead; we were nearly to the water's edge now. "The river offers healing energy—the lifeforce of *all* Egypt."

As we came upon the embankment, the way became more treacherous, and Zahra began to stumble over large, slippery rocks and thick marshy soil. I reached out a hand to her, again, hoping she would accept my assistance.

She declined once more and took another step by herself. The slick grass sent her tumbling forward; I lunged to catch her and stopped her before her dress could be stained with mud.

She gripped my arms tightly as she regained her balance.

"Thank you," she uttered.

When I offered her my hand one more time, she took it.

I located a clean, dry patch of land at the bank of the river and sat, motioning for her to do the same. She swept her dress down behind her and slowly lowered herself to the ground, removing her sandals shortly after.

Since we were far from the village now, I softened the glow of my skin and cast a wisp of magic into the air above us, willing it to burn like a flame suspended in time. Zahra's gaze locked onto it and she watched it intently for several moments, as if she were mesmerized by its enchanting dance.

"What happened earlier," I started, glancing at her. "Please do not think any less of me for it." Her gaze broke from the flame and she looked at me. "I did what I had to do. I did not mean to..." I stopped myself again. "Those men sealed their fates when they chose to harm you."

"I do not think any less of you," she replied, stretching her legs to dip her toes into the river. The hem of her dress kissed the water's surface and the firelight overhead cast amber radiance upon her ankles.

Nut's children twinkled above us, frolicking joyfully across rolling hills of a cosmic meadow dotted with blooms.

Zahra remained quiet and so did I, as I could not think of what to say. Watching her enjoy the life-giving water of the river as it soaked away her tension had me captivated. She seemed truly at peace, as I had never seen her before.

Rustling reeds caught my ear and I turned my attention to the sound. There was a long, drawn out hissing, and I veered sharply around, startling Zahra.

"What is it?" she asked. I held out a flattened hand to quiet her.

Then I heard it again—the hiss—but I could not hone in on the location. Grass waved in the evening breeze and the reeds clacked more loudly, masking the strange noise completely.

Wet earth shifted and a scaly black creature emerged, its eyes as yellow as fire and its purple tongue flicking, tasting the air. It slithered closer and reared up, hissing fiercely. The cobra forced open its hood and began to weave from side to side rhythmically while its golden eyes focused on me.

Zahra shrieked and scrambled to her feet.

"Stay behind me!" I roared, coming to my knees.

A wild beast would never harm a god. They were our servants, and the cobra—offspring of the benevolent goddess, Wadjet—was no exception. Yet the snake threatened me.

It struck like a whip, but I caught it midair, before its fangs could pierce my flesh. The snake writhed and my fingers could barely retain a firm grasp on its slick scales. How was it so strong!?

"Be careful, Horus!" Zahra cried out from behind me.

"Stay... back," I grunted.

The cobra snapped at me over and over again, each clack of its jaws forcing my grip to loosen, my hands to weaken.

I clenched my teeth and squeezed the beast harder, forcing all my magic and strength into keeping a hold on it. A small set of black horns sprouted from its head and I could not take my focus off them as they stretched and grew.

I recognized the flat, seared tops of those ears...

"Set!"

A serpentine smile stretched across its face. "You have explaining to do, Nephew!" it hissed. The cobra's face morphed into that of my uncle Set's and I jolted, letting go of the creature instantly.

A deep, tearing sensation rattled me and I lost all control over my magic, involuntarily releasing the sand and elements of my form into the air to be carried away by the wind.

Warped images of Zahra shuttered in and out as she spoke indistinct words to which I could not respond. My entire being was shrinking away, leaving an emptiness behind that made me disoriented and weak. Red and white stars flashed, consuming me with blinding light. Then my vision faded, and a loud humming sound enveloped me.

A new feeling struck my mind and heart, mercilessly chipping away to reveal a weakness I did not even know I had.

Fear.

I awoke in a dark chamber with not so much as a hairline

crack of light stealing through the shadows. The place was poisoned with unnatural silence, and the air was as still as death. I shifted in place, but my arms and legs moved as one, accompanied by a loud, unsettling clinking of metal.

"We find before us the son of Osiris, ruler of the underworld, and Isis, protector of mother and child, the Sky God, Horus," the voice boomed all around, echoing from walls I could not see.

A searing flash of white light illuminated the place, forcing me to squeeze my eyes shut.

"What is the meaning of this!?" I called out, but my moving lips released no words; it was as if my voice had been stolen from me.

"You will speak when you are spoken to," the voice added.

As my eyes acclimated to the lighting, I began to see my surroundings. Heavy metal chains bound my wrists and ankles. I tried to move but could not budge; the iron radiated with heat and a reddish hue, indicating it had been enchanted with powerful magic.

A deep chasm held me, with walls so high, I could barely see the top. Out-of-focus faces of other gods looked down upon me, as if I were a boar captured in a pit trap. Like predators, all eyes were locked on me.

With my falcon sight, I saw deep-set expressions of disappointment and judgment wrinkling their beastly faces.

"You have been sentenced to court to be tried for your intolerable behavior on Earth," Ra announced, his golden headdress coming into view as he loomed over the edge of the pit. It was he who had spoken moments ago.

Bastet stood near him, her eyes solemn and weary as

she looked off to the side, trying not to stare at me.

My mother was nowhere to be seen.

"What have I done!?" I called out to the crowd, but again, my voice had been muted. The shackles! I glared at them. They must have cursed me not to speak. I struggled to free myself, but I could not wriggle my hands out.

A bout of worry struck me as I realized Zahra had been left alone by the river's edge, and no one was there to light her way back in the dark of night. If she were to be harmed a second time, I would—

"What have you done?" a rigid, hoarse voice repeated.

The earth trembled and cracked. Red smoke drifted up from a fissure that had opened in the ground several feet in front of me. The faintly glowing smoke rose and began to take the shape of a familiar being.

White and red stars ignited within it and Set manifested from the puff of color, his boney fingers firmly grasping a tall *was scepter*.

"I am quite certain they would all like to know what it is you have done," he continued, looking down at me with a villainous sneer. His fangs shimmered even in the low light, and his purple tongue flicked against them as he spoke. "Let us begin by reciting the Oath of the Gods."

I strained, attempting to move so that I could watch him as he circled me, but the weight of the chains made it nearly impossible to change position.

"None shall alter one's fate," Set began. "None shall favor another. None shall undo others' work. None shall cause death. None shall grant life to the dead."

That feeling pumped through my veins again—the

uncomfortable, unsettling one that had forced a wave of weakness to crash over me. My heart thumped in my rib cage and sickness stirred in my gut. I swallowed, but a kind of tightness made it difficult and it felt like something squeezed my throat.

"Would you care to tell the court how many laws you have broken, Horus?" Set asked, jabbing the long, twisted scepter at my face until the two sharp prongs at the base threatened my eyes.

"I have done nothing wrong," I defended. The words came out this time, though they were quiet and did not resonate through the chasm like Set's and Ra's had.

"You lie!" Set twirled his staff and swung it, striking me on the side of the face. A piercing ache resonated through me and a buzzing sound swelled in my ears.

The feeling made no sense.

Gods did not feel pain, and yet an unnerving twinge pulsated where Set had hit me.

"Shall I begin, my king?" Set asked, glancing up toward Ra.

Ra tipped his head.

"It should be known to all attending," Set started, looking up at the other gods watching from the top of the pit, "that young Horus has committed an atrocious offense. He murdered a mortal!"

A loud gasp swirled through the chasm as all the gods, except Ra, drew back in disbelief. Ra remained as still and expressionless as one of the statues outside Zahra's temple.

"It was an accident," I replied. "You know nothing of the circumstances."

Ra's eyes narrowed with curiosity. "Then tell us, Horus, of the circumstances. To kill is to break a governing law in the sacred oath by which all immortals must abide."

I mustered every ounce of strength, took in a deep breath, and heaved myself up off the ground, clambering to catch my balance; the weight of the massive chains made me hunch.

"I did not deliberately kill the mortal," I began, and then cleared my throat. "He and his associates were guilty of harming one of your very own God's Wives." I looked up toward Ra. "The man took a priestess from your temple, beat her, and then marred her face with a knife. I sought justice for her, but it was not my intention to *kill*."

Ra's expression changed into a neutral one.

"Oh, dear nephew," Set croaked, "accident or not, you did, in fact, murder a human, and thus, you have also altered one's fate. Perhaps, even, the fate of many. But... those are not necessarily the most serious of the crimes you have committed."

What more had I—

"You must tell your king *why* those men attacked his poor wife to begin with. Tell everyone, Horus, what you did to one of Ra's revered wives." He snarled beneath his breath and I could swear I saw a smile crack his lips just before he turned away and his sparkling cloak blocked my line of sight.

I tried to conjure an excuse but... there was none. Had Set been watching me from the very beginning!? How did he know about the mark?

My chains felt ten times heavier and I was brought to my knees suddenly. The hard crack of my legs against the floor sent a ripple of what had to have been *pain* straight through me.

Set twisted around to face me again. "Ah! You were eager to defend yourself, but now that you have been questioned, you have become silent. My lord," he genuflected toward Ra, "young Horus secretly covets the head priestess of your temple."

Flame exploded from Ra's eyes and all the gods took a step back as he leaned over the pit to look down at me. "Is this true!?" His voice shook the earth.

I could not lie.

I could not tell the truth, either.

I would be condemned, regardless.

"Your precious wife has been corrupted and forever marked by this foolish young god," Set growled. "Behold the mark of betrayal, my king." Set waved his staff and a swirling cloud of imagery took shape, revealing to the crowd the exact moment in time when I had given Zahra the tattoo, and when she had decided to hide it.

The fire of Ra's existence began to seep out of his physical form, consuming him in a blaze of heat and vibrant flashes of color.

"He branded her as his own," Set added, raising his voice to combat the angry rumble coming from Ra, "and attempted to use and convert your disciple for his own wicked deeds."

The darkness retreated back against the walls of the pit as Ra lifted his arm up overhead, allowing his fire to burn so brightly that it nearly singed my eyes.

"I have reached my verdict!" Ra bellowed. "Let this be a lesson to all gods, and to all mortals who have or desire to take part in this blasphemy. Horus, son of Osiris and Isis, you will be stripped of your power. No replacement will be assigned to your duties in your absence."

"But the people need a sky god," I huffed, fighting to breathe as the chains crushed me under their weight.

Set approached from behind and jabbed me in the back with his scepter. "You should have thought about that before you became involved with a priestess of Ra!" He came around to the front of me, leaned over, wrapped his pointy, gaunt fingers around my necklace and–

"NO!" I screamed.

He yanked it from my neck.

"You will not require this anymore," he snarled, crushing it in his hands. Shards of red crystal scattered across the floor like grains of sand; each particle exploded into dust and drifted up out of the chasm and into the cosmos.

Extreme heat washed over me as Ra loomed over the edge of the pit and pointed. "I sentence you to exile!" he boomed.

Thunder crashed and the floor quaked violently beneath me, sending me onto my side as complete darkness swallowed me whole and I became weightless in the air. The chains vanished and I fell into nothingness. Shadows gnawed at my flesh, siphoning magic from my veins until I had been drained dry of any sense of purpose.

A terrible instinct took over and I opened my mouth to cry out. The sound of clashing lightning drummed upon my ears until I thought they might burst, and my head throbbed with intense pressure. A hissing sound resonated through the darkness, but I could not focus on it once my body hit the ground and I howled in pain.

"Horus!" Zahra grabbed me by my shoulders and shook

me. "Horus!"

My eyes eased opened and I blinked, trying to focus on her face, which was lit only by pale moonlight. For the first time ever, my skin excreted sweat, and the sensation made me hot and cold at the same time. A surge of sharpness drilled through my forearm and I looked down to find two perfectly symmetrical holes oozing blood.

"You are bleeding!" Zahra screamed.

"What... ha-ppened...?" I blinked several times, but everything became blurry and an intense, ill feeling swelled in my stomach. "Za-hra?" My mind thought the words correctly, but my mouth would not speak them without slurring them together.

I heard Zahra call for help once, just before all sounds around me became garbled.

Every inch of me was on fire—as if Ra's rage had consumed me and I was being burned alive by the sun...

14

SOMEONE grasped my shoulders firmly.

"Horus. Horus, can you hear me?" Zahra's voice was muffled and distant. "Please, wake up."

My eyes would barely open; I forced them to, and overwhelming brightness stung my retinas and made me recoil. I raised my arm to try to shield myself from Ra's vengeful rays, but the motion sent a riveting twinge of pain through me.

"Zahra?" I spoke her name hoarsely and with great pain, as my throat burned and the fragile skin on my dry, chapped lips cracked.

"He is awake!" she called out.

Everything ached as it had never ached before. Taking in a breath made my ribs sting and sent a wave up my spine that made me cringe.

Was *this* pain?

It had to be.

We had not been acquainted long, but it had already overstayed its welcome.

A low wavering voice, which had an air of kindness to

it, said, "The gods must be on your side, young man."

"I-I doubt it," I muttered; speaking was just as uncomfortable the second time.

I turned—the action made my neck hurt—and looked toward the old man approaching. He hobbled closer to the bed I had been laid out on and paused to stand beside me, scratching his fluffy grey beard with his wrinkly, age-spotted fingers.

I bit down hard, clenching my teeth together involuntarily as both Zahra and the old stranger helped me sit up. She shoved a fluffy sack of padding behind me for support and then retrieved a small clay bowl of water and brought it to me. Her steady hands lifted it toward my lips and I leaned my head down and took a sip.

I coughed after a splash shot toward my airway and sent me into a spasm. The act of drinking was unfamiliar—gods neither ate nor drank since we were wholly sustained by magic—but I was compelled to try.

A moment after I had choked, I composed myself, cleared my throat, and then motioned for Zahra to bring the water again. This time, I was successful, and the gentle liquid soothed and cooled my throat and lips.

"Th-thank you," I uttered, releasing my weight back against the cushion behind me.

My vision was clearing up now and the sunlight creeping in through the nearby window did not burn quite as much anymore. Zahra brought a damp cloth up to my face and patted it across my forehead, providing some relief from the steaming-hot sweat seeping from my pores.

"Where are we?" I asked, glancing at her first and then

at the old man.

"In my home. I am a doctor," he replied. "Do you know who you are?"

Who I am?

"I am—" I stopped myself. Was I allowed to tell this mortal, or would the gods come for me again? I cleared my throat and replied, "Yes. I know who I am. And that is Zahra, my—"

"Wife," she blurted.

I gazed at her, confused, and a comforting, reassuring smile lit up her face.

"I am certain he will be fine, doctor," she continued, approaching to take my hand between hers. Her skin was exceptionally soft and warm, and I instinctively squeezed her fingers gently.

"It really is a miracle that you survived," the doctor added with a shake of his head. "You must be strong and favored by the gods. Your wife came to me just in time. Had she been a jackal's howl later, you would not have survived that cobra's bite."

Would not have survived!?

Would the gods have allowed me to die?

Was it their intention to? Was it... *Set's* intention!?

Hatred swelled in my heart and I angrily pushed up from the bed.

Pain disabled me and I reeled back. Looking down at the bandage wrapped around my wound, I noticed my golden armbands were missing. Zahra appeared embarrassed by my observation.

"I gave them to him as payment for his help," she said.

"I am a very poor man, my boy," the doctor added. "Medicine is an expensive practice."

The idea of having to give away my belongings simply to pay someone to save my life seemed foreign and inhumane, but I also knew that the mortal realm was a difficult one, and that the cost of living was constantly on the rise.

"I understand, and I thank you for your help. I wish to leave now."

"You are still weak," the doctor said. "I suggest you rest until you feel well enough to carry on—at least until your fever has subsided. I did not save you only to allow you to wander off and get your wound infected, or worse." He chuckled and the raspy laugher comforted me in some way. "You are welcome to stay until then."

His heartfelt offer was appealing and I accepted it. After all, I had ignored Bastet's words of warning and now found myself struggling with the aftermath of a mortal wound.

I was not as invincible as I had once thought.

"You have been asleep for two days," Zahra informed me after the doctor had left the room. She sat on the edge of my bed and clasped her hands in her lap. "If the doctor had not been traveling home on the road near the river, I fear I may not have been able to save you."

The coincidences were many, and it led me to believe that at least a few gods wanted me to stay alive. Now was not the time to wonder who.

"I told the doctor I was your wife, else he would not have allowed us to stay here together," she said quietly and very matter-of-factly. "Now you must tell me what happened to you at the riverside." She turned to face me. There were dark shadows around her eyes, indicating she had lost much sleep in the wake of these events. "I could not see everything in the faint moonlight, but a snake struck you. I should like to believe a god would not have been harmed by such a creature."

"You are correct in thinking the gods cannot and should not be harmed in such a way." I licked my dry lips and then delicately traced the wrapping on my arm with my fingertips. "But I am no longer a god..."

Zahra let out a yelp of surprise and her eyes grew wide. "How can that be? How can you no longer be a god!?"

"Because of my actions, Ra stripped me of my powers and forced me into mortality." I swallowed hard and felt a lump in my throat. "I am as human as you now."

"Because of the man who died? But... can you not return and beg for the gods' mercy!? How could you have done such wrong!? I cannot believe it."

"I committed murder," I whispered. "The most offensive, utterly intolerable act that there is. And... I showed preference to you."

Her brow furrowed. "You *protected* me in a time of dire need! How can a god be punished for showing kindness!? It makes no sense at all."

"Gods are not to favor and not to kill—two grave offenses that cannot be forgiven. Ra has exiled me from the Palace of the Gods forever, and that is why you sit with me now and must tend my human wounds."

Zahra looked away for a moment and back at me. "Does

this mean you will live a mortal life and... die a mortal death?" Sadness shaped her face.

"Yes." I would not begin my mortal life with a lie.

She covered her mouth with her hands and shuddered. "No," sounded beneath her breath.

"Zahra?" I spoke quietly, lifting my hand to caress her arm. "Although I have much to learn, I do know that a mortal life is fleeting. If this is to be my life from here forward, then I will do all I can to make it valuable and to bring reprieve to yours in any way possible." My hand drifted down, and the warmth of her skin compelled me to entwine my fingers with hers. "I promised to protect you, Zahra, and I will keep that promise, even now."

She appeared both surprised and pleased by my words, and seeing her smile brought lightness to my heart. It felt good, as if I had said the right thing and—

Zahra forked the fingers of her free hand through my hair, and suddenly leaned down close enough that I felt her breath upon my lips. Our eyes locked and she remained there, still, gazing thoughtfully at me as her fingers tangled through my hair. The sensation was new and pleasant.

Then *my* heart started to race.

What was I feeling, and how did such a small act make my breath tremble? It was not discomfort. It also was not fear.

Her gaze flitted between my eyes and my lips. Then she sucked in a breath and backed away suddenly, withdrawing both hands and looking off to the side as if she had made a mistake.

"I am sorry, my lord," she spoke. Redness flushed her face.

An unsettling feeling of disappointment roiled through me, though I did not exactly understand why.

Then I felt inclined to tell her, "I am no longer your lord, Zahra."

She did not reply.

The day wore on, and while I rested in bed, waiting for evening to come, when travel back to the temple would be easier, I pondered what would become of me now that I had to consider the repercussions of having a mortal body and a shortened life.

How many years did I have? Where would I live?

Would or *could* Zahra stay with me?

Did she even wish to?

I had witnessed men working with masonry, tending crops, and raising livestock. All those jobs required years of expertise and training, neither of which I had.

With some help, I got up from bed and looked out the window, to the pasture not far from the doctor's home. The grass had yellowed overnight, and the blazing sun cast rays substantially hotter than usual. Zahra wiped sweat from her face several times, dunking a cloth into a bowl of water and patting herself down with it. She did the same for me next, though it offered only marginal relief from the scorching heat.

"It has never been this unbearable before," she said, fanning herself with a thick papyrus sheet.

Without me there to control the sky, influence the clouds, or change the winds, the currents became stagnant and the air dry. From what I could see through the window, nearby bodies of water were rapidly evaporating.

Ra declared my role would not be filled after my expulsion, but the people did not deserve to suffer because of my wrongdoing.

The sound of a woman clearing her throat made me turn my head away from the window.

The doctor's wife, who had hair as grey as ash and age spots speckling her wrinkly skin, stood in the threshold of the tiny room with a pile of cloth between her hands. "Our son passed years ago in a fishing accident," she said, "and we no longer need this. My husband suggested you cover that mark upon your chest, as it may stir trouble in the village."

She had meant my birth tattoo.

I did not know what to say; I did not feel the need to cover the mark, as it was the last remaining evidence of my godly birthright.

"Thank you," Zahra answered for me, smiling gratefully and taking the clothes from the old woman. "We appreciate your generosity. I will see to it that he changes."

The doctor's wife left and Zahra helped dress me with the long, thick, white tunic. The fabric was heavy but allowed air to pass through easily. It was extremely itchy and irritated my skin, but Zahra insisted I would become acquainted with it over time.

I scratched my head and scowled at the unusual greasiness of my hair. My body exuded a new and unsavory, pungent scent, and from my chin sprouted tiny, stiff hairs that were prickly and rough. I did not like them at all.

Evening approached, and the doctor and his wife gave us an oil lamp and a small loaf of bread, and then saw us off.

"Safe journey," he said.

Zahra bowed to the doctor and his wife and we left together.

"Where will I stay?" I asked, holding the lamp at hip level because my arms were still weak.

"You will stay with me," Zahra said in a hushed tone, "in the temple."

"What if it angers Ra?"

Zahra stopped walking and turned to face me. "What more can he do? He has already taken everything from you. Should he attempt anything more than that, he would likely break the same sacred oath that he claims you did."

She was right. Ra had already stolen my immortality and my magic. What more could he do, short of murder?

"You will stay with me," she continued, "until I can find you work and a safe place to live."

Days ago, I soared amongst the ibises, and now I had to consider taking up mortal work and finding a home. It was all so very new and strange to me. My only hope was that with Zahra's help, I could survive even a short while on this earth.

I agreed with her suggestion and we continued our way back to the village, the sun setting quickly at our heels and the moon eager to rise.

A flock of geese flew overhead, honking sporadically, just as the last stroke of purple horizon drained from the sky. I craned my neck back to watch as they passed by, each member of the formation falling in and out of line frequently and then overcorrecting to right themselves. They were disoriented and should have returned to their nests hours ago.

"Something is wrong," I said, feeling grave discomfort flow through me as I watched the youngest goose tumble out of the sky and into the boughs of a palm. "The birds are lost without me."

"There is nothing you can do now," Zahra said, reaching to take the lamp. "Come. We are nearly there."

After checking to be sure that no other wives were wandering outside the temple or in the main hall, she spirited me inside to her room. She asked me to wait while she went to inform the other wives of her return.

I sat at the edge of her bed, unsettled and frustrated at what I had experienced thus far. Unbearable heat. Bewildered birds. With wells and ponds shrinking at an accelerated rate, a drought was imminent.

When Zahra returned, there was a deep frown weighing upon her lips.

"What happened?" I asked, standing.

"I did not want to disturb them all so I only woke Betresh, as she does not sleep as soundly as the others. Betresh informed me that there has been talk of the Sky God's wrath," she started, her expression becoming even more forlorn. "She says the villagers speak of murder by the hand of a god. I am afraid they are referring to you, Horus."

The witness—the survivor from my fit with Zahra's assailants—he must have gone forth and done *exactly* what I had demanded of him.

A demand I now regretted.

"We must call you by another name," she said.

I felt like a complete and utter fool for my arrogance, as now my very name had become a curse upon me.

"What shall I use? I do not have another name," I replied.

She sat on the edge of her bed and heaved a sigh. A muffled groan escaped her mouth and she raised her arm to eye level. "The sun was so bright that it scalded me this morning," she said with a scowl, while gazing at the inflamed and reddened flesh. "I shall have to apply a salve to cool the burning." Then her gaze shot toward me and she grinned. "Wait! I have it!"

"Have what?"

"A name for you." She stood and took a step closer to me. "Horakhty."

I did not know how I felt about it, but I remained silent so as to not upset her with my indecision.

"It means 'rising sun,'" she clarified, beaming. "I cannot believe I did not think of it before. It is what you are. Fallen from the Palace of the Gods, but risen to live as one amongst us, you have been granted rebirth, like the rising sun."

Horakhty...?

Her rationale made perfect sense, and the name no longer sounded awkward and strange as I moved my lips to form it silently to myself, and then once aloud. "Horakhty."

"Yes." Zahra clasped her hands together and bit her lip. "I believe it will serve you well."

I wiped my arm across my forehead to sweep away the sweat and grimaced at the throbbing pain lingering from the snakebite. I had stumbled my way back to the Temple of Ra with the priestess by my side, the scorching Egyptian sun glaring even as it drifted beneath the horizon, and mortal sweat stinging my eyes.

Although I had been stripped of all magic and condemned

to a new and fragile body, I had suddenly become a “rising sun.”

15

We had only been away for a couple of days and, already, people had begun to spread rumors of the gods exacting revenge on those who had failed to pay their dues. While speaking with patrons in the very early morning after our return, Zahra overheard stories of extreme heat killing livestock and of birds abandoning their young in droves because of a sudden famine. Trees wilted while crops shriveled and farmers lost their livelihoods seemingly overnight.

The whittling man who had been with Zahra's assailant had already spread word of my deed, and the fear of a god's wrath spread like wildfire across the village.

I sat on a small wooden stool in Zahra's room while she was at work at a table beside me. "I am sorry this happened to you," she said, crushing vivid green herbs together with a mortar and pestle, just how the doctor had instructed her to before we left. The pungent, bitter powder could be mixed with hot water to make a drink that would calm pain temporarily, or with liquid fat to create a paste for the wound, should swelling or redness continue. The side effects of ingestion were drowsiness, but seeing how I needed the rest, I did not object to its use.

“I will do all I can to make you comfortable, until you recover.” She poured some powder into a clay bowl and set it aside, then added a small amount of heated, rendered goat fat to the remaining mixture. With a gentle stroke of her fingers, Zahra painted the salve over the puncture wounds. She withdrew a stretch of linen from nearby and wrapped it around my arm several times to keep the ointment in place and protect it from the elements. The salve stung, but much less severely than it had during my first experience with it.

The other wives would awaken soon, but they would not be made aware of my taking up residence in the temple. Zahra had put together a makeshift place for me last night, and I slept on the floor near the far corner of her chamber. I awoke in much pain, with sharp discomfort in my neck and spine. The floor of the temple was composed of sand and stone, and my bedding meager, at best, but it was all she could offer me, and I was grateful to not have been sleeping outside without cover. The temple also provided some defense against bugs and other night terrors while granting relief from the staggering heat.

My newly developed sense of smell took in strong, unfamiliar scents. Incense was potent and noticeable. The frankincense she used to purify the temple was bright and earthy with a warm, comforting undertone.

“I am happy you survived,” Zahra whispered, setting the pestle on the table and then kneeling at my feet and sitting back on her heels; I occupied the only stool in the room. “I was afraid you would be lost to the underworld.” She clasped her hands together in her lap and looked down at them. "Though I wish the other gods would have helped you."

"I believe they did," I replied quietly. "Else, I likely would not be alive at all."

I slipped off the seat so that I could sit beside her, and a rush of another new scent tickled my nostrils. I liked this one very much. It was flowery and sweet, and it reminded me of early spring, when blossoms opened toward the sky and youth was in the air.

"Jasmine," she whispered.

I was caught off-guard by her comment and stared back her.

"I noticed you sniffing with bewilderment. That smell is jasmine." She lifted an arm toward her table and dragged over a small, colorful glass vial with golden accents and a dainty stopper. She pulled off the stopper, and it made an oddly satisfying sound.

The flowery smell, though pleasant at first, overwhelmed me in concentration and I let out a nervous laugh. "I understand. Now please cover it. What you are wearing is more than enough."

She smiled. It was a sweet, content smile that made her eyes narrow and her cheeks rise. It was a beautiful and happy smile that gave me a shared sense of peace and joy.

"The smell of jasmine pleases me," I replied, grinning back at her.

Her expression straightened and she sucked in a sharp breath. She came hastily to her feet, placed the perfume back onto her table, and then reached for the bowl of remaining medicine powder. "I will prepare the drink," she said, her voice shaky.

"What did I say?" I asked, standing just as quickly. "Zahra?"

She glanced up at me and tipped her head. "I will get you warm water," she added, and then hurried out of the room.

"Zahra." I could not raise my voice, for fear of being heard, but I called to her hoarsely anyway. What had I said or done to make her leave in such a hurry?

I flopped down onto the floor again and sat with my legs crossed, looking down at the bandage on my arm. It was no ordinary snake that had poisoned me. It was Set. My destiny had been preordained, but now I wondered if he had known something I had not, for he was eager to force it from my grasp.

I had not been in thought for more than a moment when a commotion caught my ear. It came from the main hall and involved Zahra and a few other wives. I crept closer to the threshold of her room to listen; it was off to the side of the main hall, but I still had to take care not to be seen.

"Is she not with you!?" the other wife asked frantically. "Please, tell us she is with you, Zahra!"

"No. No, she is not," I heard Zahra respond. I inched closer to the threshold so I could see out. "Were you not with her last night!?"

The other woman lowered her face and let out a pained groan. "Oh, we have failed you, Priestess. Nephiri went missing just before you arrived back yesterday evening. She went in search of you."

"And you let her go!? Alone!?" Zahra shouted.

“W-we tried to stop her, but...” one wife replied.

“We are not to leave after dusk!” the other defended. “You know this, Zahra! And yet you abandoned us without warning! What were we to do without your guidance!?”

“After you returned, we were certain she had found you,” interjected the other woman, who was nearly out of breath, “and foolishly assumed she was in your care for the night.” She clasped her hands together and bowed. “Please do not fret; Lord Ra will surely guide her back to us soon.”

“Ra will do nothing!” Zahra snarled. “He does not care about us.”

Both wives gasped.

“Priestess!” they cried in tandem. “What are you saying!?”

A look of fear wrinkled Zahra’s face and she grimaced. “Forget what I have said. We must find Nephiri immediately. Dangers await her in the city, and she is young and frail. I will not allow her to be taken from us.” She took in a deep breath and exhaled loudly. “I hope it is not too late to find her.”

Poor Zahra had lost much sleep over the past few days, and caring for me left her exhausted. Dark shadows colored her eyes still, and even her enraged tone of voice was less formidable than it had been in the past.

I, too, was tired and still learning how to cope with my weak mortal flesh. But something inside me sparked to life, and I knew in my human heart and mind that I *had* to do anything and everything within my power to help.

I came out of hiding and entered the main hall. “I will find her.”

Both women looked toward me, shrieked, and backed away.

"Do not fear me," I said to them. "Your priestess has been treating a severe wound I acquired." I lifted my bandaged arm toward them. "I know this city well. If anyone can find the girl, it will be me."

Zahra's eyes widened, and for a moment she appeared as though she might scold me with a hundred curses. But a stretch of silence passed and she looked toward the other wives and said, "He speaks the truth. Though we have been in brief contact, I remain pure and true to my faith. I have been caring for him because..." She cleared her throat. "I owe him a debt for saving my life."

Both women held their breaths in awe.

"He does, in fact, know this village very well, and I will put my trust in him to find dear Nephiri and bring her back to us."

Zahra found me a cloak with which I could cover my pale hair. She equipped me with a satchel containing a cask of water and a few small things to eat, and then I left the temple to begin my search.

I began in the marketplace, asking every man, woman, and child if they had heard or seen anything concerning the young priestess.

I proceeded this way through the village, the majority of my time wasted on dead ends and misinformation. I swept every road, alley, and place of dwelling, and asked everyone I could, until only the temples of the gods remained.

It took a great deal of pride and courage to gather the nerve to enter the temples of the other gods, but I could leave no stone unturned.

Where would a child of such a young age have thought to look for Zahra?

I continued to ask around, but either no one knew a thing, or the ones who thought they had, described a girl with different features.

I gazed up at the horizon and watched brilliant oranges and blues dance below the falling orb of amber fire. The thought of leaving Nephiri to fend for herself one more night terrified me. The darkness would surely devour her, subjecting her to terrors no child should have to endure. Soon, dusk would spirit away the light and Nut would return to her place amongst the stars. A great seed of doubt began to sprout in me.

What would Zahra think of me if I could not locate the youngest and most innocent of all the God's Wives?

I asked the attendants of each temple, and cautiously entered those which had been left unattended, but found nothing. The only temple that remained was that of my mother, Isis—the goddess and protector of women and children.

As much as I despised the thought of begging my negligent mother to assure Nephiri's safe return, I convinced myself that it had to be done.

When I arrived there, though, the Temple of Isis was woefully quiet and the candles had already been extinguished inside. Or perhaps they had not been lit at all earlier in the day. Many of the temples had been hastily abandoned since the abrupt drought had stifled the city, as the priests and priestesses could not afford to feed themselves while the villagers scrambled to salvage what foods they could for their own families.

I withdrew a chunk of flint from the supplies Zahra had given me and used it to spark and ignite one of the lamps at the threshold of the temple. I was chasing sunlight now, and Nut and her children would arrive at any moment.

I entered the temple and headed toward the grandiose statue of my mother which sat in the center, surrounded by the familiar pool of lotus blossoms.

The flowers were shriveled and decaying, their wispy petals drifting through the water like threads of rotted flesh. The pool had been tinted an unsettling shade of red, and as I carried the lamp closer to the water's edge, a dark scarlet smudge on the stones made my lungs seize.

My body stiffened with fear; I recognized the ghastly color.

Holding the lamp as firmly as I could with my shaking hand, I knelt by the edge of the pool and lifted the light out over the water.

A small, pale body floated there.

I set the lamp aside and climbed into the shallow pond, wading toward the center as swiftly as my feeble mortal legs could carry me over slippery, algae-covered stone and decomposing flowers.

I flipped Nephiri over, scooped her up into my arms, and waded back to the edge to lie her down on dry stone. A large gash marred her forehead; she must have slipped on the neglected pathway. Her skin was pallid and her body as frigid as the night.

I pulled myself out of the pool, crawled over to the child, and then leaned down to her face to listen.

Silence.

I pressed an ear to her chest and it was as if her ice-cold body had suddenly inflicted the same condition upon me. A shiver ran up my spine and I shuddered at the hollow quiet in her ribcage.

She was dead.

How long had her body been here!? Had she come to pray for Zahra's safe return!?

I glared up at the statue of my mother and hissed through my gritted teeth.

"How dare you take an innocent child without remorse," I seethed. "In your own temple, no less." My pulse thumped and my chest tightened as a squeezing ache ripped through me. Molten anger flushed through my body and the urge to tear a stone from the water's edge and smash the face from my mother's sculpture beckoned to me.

She did not deserve her servants.

But there was no time for resentment. I had to return to Zahra before the night became too dark for me to see my way back. I could not carry the lamp and the body simultaneously.

I slid my hands beneath Nephiri and then gently lifted her into my arms. Every step taken with the child's body dangling in my grasp pierced my heart like a new snakebite—fangs tearing into flesh, pumping painful venom and debilitating toxins through my body—empowering me with adrenaline as I rushed back to the Temple of Ra.

"He found her!" Zahra shouted as I neared the entryway. Her voice was full of hope as she hurried toward me.

"Where was she? Is she—" She yelped and cupped her mouth. "No. Oh, no. No!" She shook her head and entwined her hands together near her face. "Wh-what happened!? Where did you find her!?"

"I was too late," I uttered.

I said nothing more as I carried the body past her, into the temple, and laid it at the feet of Ra's statue.

Zahra began to sob and the other God's Wives joined her in a choir of mournful clamor. I retrieved a decorative linen from Zahra's room and laid it down halfway across Nephiri's body, covering much of the faded bloodstains that tarnished her white dress.

Intense sadness swelled in my chest, and I retreated to Zahra's room.

It was my fault Zahra had disappeared from the temple.

My fault Nephiri sought Isis for guidance.

For the second time, I had brought death to another...

16

I STOOD alone in Zahra's room, leaning against a wall, fighting to tune out the terrible sounds of suffering resonating from the hall where I had laid down Nephiri's body.

Unyielding sorrow lanced my heart and it was as if an invisible force whispered to me of my uselessness—mocking me and burrowing into my mind until a remarkable new, terrifying power made my muscles weak.

I fell to my knees and crumpled over, covering my face with my hands as my body shook with emotion and sickness pooled in my stomach.

And I cried.

I tried to resist, but no amount of courage could stop the tears from escaping my eyes. These were not the same tears I had shed once before. Neither from angst and sulking, nor because of something Ra had denied me.

These tears wounded me from the inside out. They made my body weak and my mind swirl with regrets.

Warm fingers rested on my shoulder, and the heat of embarrassment flushed through me. Would Zahra view me as pathetic for my outburst?

She knelt beside me.

I tried to speak, but the sharp pain in my throat made me do so with great difficulty.

"W-what is this that brings me to my knees?" I uttered, wiping my damp cheeks. "What makes my chest quake and my lungs feel squeezed? That crushes me until saltwater pours from my eyes?" I sniffed hard and coughed.

Zahra took a deep breath and placed her fingers at the base of my scalp. "Pain," she replied softly, her voice tainted with grief. "It has many names, and it is different for us all."

I glanced toward her and shook my head. "I do not wish to feel this anymore. Why would Ra force such an unbearable punishment upon me? I-I would rather be dead than—"

"Human?" Zahra finished my sentence.

I nodded.

"Humanity has many faults, as we are slaves to emotion, but it is what makes us who we are and sets us apart from... what you once were. A world of finite things can be unforgiving, but it also offers moments of unimaginable joy. It is those moments—their brevity—that make the pain worth enduring."

She spoke with the wisdom and poise of a goddess, and her words comforted me and caused my tears to slow.

"I had thought for a moment," she added, "that I had lost you to the serpent by the river. For two days, I questioned my purpose in this world. But then you returned to me—a mortal body of flesh and blood—and I gained renewed hope and faith in my being here."

"Even though I have brought nothing but famine and

death?" I asked. "Ra is angry, and my actions have spurred him to punish you and your people for harboring me."

"My decisions were my own," she replied. "Come. It is late and we must get sleep." She pointed toward the pile of palm boughs and cotton in the corner, which I had slept upon the previous night.

"What of Nephiri?" I walked over to the bedding and shuffled through it, hoping to make it more comfortable.

"In the morning, her body will be delivered to another temple, where it will be prepared for mummification over the next several weeks."

She would be judged by the jackal-faced god of the underworld, Anubis, and—if her heart proved its worthiness against the Feather of Truth—my father, Osiris, would either admit her into eternal paradise or allow her to be reincarnated.

I sat on the uncomfortable palm leaves. Zahra noticed my shuffling around the bedding and excused herself from the room.

I heard voices in the hall, some brief arguing, and then she returned with a bundle of fabric in her arms.

"You may use these blankets," she said, tossing them toward me. "The other wives have allowed me to give them to you."

"I am grateful for their generosity," I said, rubbing my fingers over the coarse wool.

"They are unhappy with my decision to house you here, but they cannot tell me otherwise, as I am the head priestess. I fear you will not be safe here for long, however."

"Safe? Why not? What do you fear may happen?"

"With all the talk of angry gods, and with the weather changing and the animals acting very strange, it will not be long before there is a surge in offerings and the patrons become desperate for relief. The Temple of Ra has never permitted sanctuary to a man before, and it should not begin now, even if—"

"Then leave this place," I said, my voice rising. The fact that she would liken *me* to an *ordinary man* was appalling, and a great disrespect after all I had done for her. "Leave the temple with me. We will begin a new life together."

She looked away and sighed, but then said nothing.

"Zahra?"

She pressed her lips thin; the silence was agonizing.

I wanted to prod her for a swift reply but thought better of myself.

"I cannot," she whispered.

I stood up from my bedding. "Why?"

"Because this temple is all I know," she said softly, her lip trembling and great distress twisting her face. "I am a priestess of Ra and nothing more."

I approached her with heavy steps and reached out to grab her by the forearms. "Zahra, do you not trust me? I may have been stripped of my power, but it does not render me useless. I *will* learn how to thrive in this world and I *will* learn how to manage my mortality. But I will find no value in this life if I cannot spend my time with you."

"It was different then." Her words barely reached my ears as she said them with her face turned to the side.

"How? How was it different then?" I tightened my grasp on her until her face rose and her tired, watery eyes met mine.

"I-I am a God's Wife," she managed through labored breaths, "and you are no longer a god."

I released her immediately. Partly out of shock and disgust, and partly because I felt that if I had continued holding on, my distress might make me squeeze too hard.

"The people will banish me if they discover I have sheltered a man in the Temple of Ra," she defended. "Then I will have nothing at all."

All the talk of betrayal from Ra and Set, and now Zahra would betray me, too? Vile, burning thoughts swirled through my mind and my body heat rose. "I sacrificed everything for you," I growled. "I lost my godly powers because of my desire to protect you, and you dare to use my mortality against me!?"

My heart beat like a falcon's wings in a storm, and my breath became shallow. I partly yearned to scream and partly yearned to cry. But all of me wanted Zahra to stay in my life. Despite the changing times, I would not let her wash me away like a petty stain.

"I made a mistake in agreeing to be your servant," she uttered beneath her breath.

Lies.

The words sounded false coming from her lips, even as her mouth tried to say them convincingly.

So instead of raising my voice again, as I had heard other angry mortals do toward one another, I reached for Zahra's hand and clasped it between mine.

"I may or may not regain my godly powers someday, but without your faith in me, I will never have the strength to carry on or to try." I brushed my fingers over the back of her hand. "What happened to Nephiri was an accident, and I will never forgive myself for it. But I refuse to step back and watch my doings drain you of your happiness. You changed on the day we touched, and... at the doctor's home, you felt something very strong when you brought your face near mine."

She used her other hand to swipe tears from her cheeks, and a small, insecure grin cracked her lips. "Nephiri was like a daughter to me," she uttered. "Losing her will make every day darker. I fear I am not strong enough to face what is to come if her passing is only the beginning of the gods' wraths."

"We will be strong together," I said, smiling at her and tipping her chin up so that I could gaze upon her better. Then I released her hand and embraced her tightly.

This time, she did not squirm, tremble, or otherwise make any attempts to escape.

She only lifted her arms ever so slowly and brought them around my back so that she could pull me even closer, and then pressed her face to my chest and wept.

17

THE MORNING heat was unbearable and I awoke sticky with sweat. The thicker bedding Zahra had made for me was far more comfortable, and my neck and back did not sting with as much pain. I poked my head out of her room and into the main hall.

"Horakhty!" one of the other wives called out.

I stared back, bewildered. It took me a moment to remember that it was the name Zahra had given me to use.

"Are you dense, Horakhty?" She scowled as I approached her. "Here." She stretched out her arm and offered a small linen satchel out to me. "Today is Market Day. Zahra has instructed me to send you out to retrieve our weekly offerings of dates and to purchase a bag of grain."

"She... did?" I looked around but did not see the head priestess anywhere.

"Yes. She is outside by the main walkway accepting offerings. See her on the way so that she may give you the temple medallion."

I did not know what she spoke of, but I carefully accepted

the bag with both hands. It was hefty and clinked when I shook it.

"I have counted every single stone and blessed carving in that bag," she said, narrowing her eyes and furrowing her brow sharply. "Go now, before Ra fully awakens and the sky burns."

I was not accustomed to taking orders, but I had to do what I could to assist them while they took a risk caring for me. Just outside the main entryway, past the massive statues of Ra—whose icy gazes seemed to be judging me even more now—I spotted Zahra carrying a basket of bread.

"Oh. You are awake. Good." She set down the basket and groaned quietly as she straightened her back. "I have been bringing in offerings all morning. Did Betresh give you the bag of stones and carvings?"

I lifted it into view.

"Good." She shifted her thick necklace and wriggled a round, flat, metal amulet out from behind it. She lifted it up over her head and handed it to me. It hung from a thin rope chain and the embellished details were stained with green tarnish. "Show this copper medallion to the shop keeper with the dates and he will know you were sent by me. If he asks, simply say we are grieving and unable to come."

"I understand."

"Thank you. I am sorry we have had to put you to work, but we do need the help. The other wives are not fond of you and wish for you to go, but I convinced them that your strength will be a great help to us for the time being."

I grinned. "It does not trouble me at all to know that I

am able to serve you in some small way."

She looked as though she may have bowed toward me but stopped herself and smiled instead. "Thank you."

I left the temple and made my way to the marketplace with the medallion hanging from my neck and the bag of stones grasped tightly in my hand. Morning light warmed the village and the sun's rays heated the air, spawning rippling mirages in the distance.

Zahra's position as high priestess made her responsible for everything that happened at the temple. She made many of the rules and, like me, she broke them. Still, she would not be able to stay with me forever, not there, at least.

The trek to the marketplace was arduous, with excessively bright sunlight stinging my eyes and overwhelming heat drawing sweat from my skin. I had to wipe my brow numerous times within a short period of time.

My sense of direction was not as keen as it had once been and locating the date salesman took longer than I had anticipated.

I found him, eventually.

"I am here to collect your offering for the Temple of Ra," I said.

The shop keeper cocked his head to the side and stared at me. "You? Why would they send you?" He glanced at my hair. "Have we met before? I seem to recognize that straw-colored hair of yours."

"I am sure we have not, as I only just arrived last night." I lifted the medallion from the collar of my tunic and showed it to him. "Head Priestess Zahra sent me because she and the other wives are grieving over the loss of one of their own and do not feel well enough to leave."

"Oh," the man said, frowning as sadness ripped the smirk from his lips. "It pains me to hear that sorry news, especially during this time of hardship for us all. May the gods of the underworld be fair." He lowered his head in silent prayer.

I did not know how to react, so I waited quietly until he lifted his face and took a deep breath.

"Let me get those for you," he said, drawing a cloth bag from beneath his table. He used a bowl to scoop a heap of dates from a basket and then poured them into the bag. He took another large scoop and added it, making the bag plump with the dried fruit. Next, he tied it tightly closed with a coarse piece of rope. "Here." He stretched an arm across his table and plopped the bag into my hands.

"Thank you." I forced a smile in an effort to seem grateful, and then left his stall in search of the grain vendor, who I had been informed did not reside on the same side of the market.

I weaved my way through the thinner-than-usual crowd and spotted a familiar image in the distance. The tapestry that resembled my falcon face hung on a post in the very back of one of the stalls, and I gravitated toward it out of curiosity.

"Hello, young man!" Aket, the tapestry salesman I had assisted on my first day on Earth, popped up from behind the table. He must have been rummaging for stock.

I acknowledged him with a partial nod.

"Are you shopping for someone in particular?" he asked, an air of excitement livening his movements. "Might you be interested in a tapestry for your family?" He gesticulated dramatically, in an effort to lure my eye to each of his products. "You are young and handsome," he said, looking me up and down briefly. "Perhaps a gift for a prospective bride?" He reached under the table for a rolled-up tapestry and unfurled it, revealing a colorful winged scarab design in what appeared to be very fine detail and quality.

"Not at this time," I responded. "I have very little with which to purchase anything today, and I have been given specific instructions on how to spend it."

"These beauties do not cost much," he said with a toothy grin. He rolled the scarab tapestry up and exchanged it for another which he unrolled before me—a lotus blossom. "Please look carefully at the workmanship."

"They are very beautiful," I responded. "But I have been ordered by the Priestess of Ra to purchase only grain and nothing more. I do apologize." Attempting to change the subject, I pointed toward the image of me. "Who is that?" I asked. "Is that the falcon-headed god whose actions brought a great many troubles upon us?"

Aket's gaze rested upon the image with great admiration. "My business has thrived because of him, and I refuse to believe that such a benevolent god would bring disaster down upon this village."

"Will you sell it?" I asked, only to test him.

"Sell it!? Never. It is my most prized piece and it brings me luck and prosperity." He swept a hand over it and brushed away a plume of dust.

"I am sure Horus appreciates your enduring support," I said. "I believe things will get better soon. If, in the future, I find myself with currency to spare, I will consider returning here to make a purchase."

"Then I thank you for your future patronage," he replied.

I proceeded to ask him for the location of the grain vendor and he graciously pointed me in the correct direction.

The grain keeper was a man of few words, and he asked me only one question: "How many bags?"

After explaining to him that I had come from the Temple of Ra, the answer became clear and he reached down to heave a large bag into his arms. He dropped it onto the table with a thud and then I passed him the satchel of stones and carvings in return.

With the heavy bag of grain flung over my shoulder and the dates in my other hand, I backtracked through the market.

There was a commotion stirring on the other side and the location of it intrigued me. I lugged my supplies back in the direction of Aket's tapestries.

I saw two men harassing the tapestry vendor behind his table. One had him by the collar of his tunic and the other was nearby, poking a finger at my portrait.

"If you do not remove it, I will," the one grasping his collar threatened.

"I-it is only an image, p-please do not be... offended by it," Aket stammered, flailing his arms in an effort to stabilize himself as the thug held him up on the tips of his toes.

The other man jerked the tapestry off its fixture, leaving threads behind, and then tossed it to the floor and stomped upon my face.

Before my brain could stop the reaction, the words, "Get away from him!" roared from my throat. I dropped the sack of grain and bag of dates at my feet. "Leave him alone!"

The man who held Aket by the collar looked at me, chuckled, and then looked away.

"I told you to leave him alone!" I took a step closer, anxiety making my heartbeat pulse fervently. I could not tell if the sweat on my brow was from the heat or from the anger throbbing through my veins.

The bigger man dropped Aket—who then fell to the ground and choked, trying to catch his breath—and bounded up onto the table, skidded off, and landed on the ground in front. He came marching toward me, glaring. His brow furrowed sharply as his gaze hung on my hair. "You are a strange and ugly boy," he said hoarsely, reaching up to pluck a hair from my head; the act made me jolt, and I knocked his hand away from my face.

"Stop!" I clenched my fists and planted my feet on the ground as firmly as I could. I did not know what I could do to help, but now that I had enraged the animal, I had to think of something.

From the corner of my eye, I saw Aket ducking down behind his table, just as the second man came out to confront me.

I blinked, and in that fleeting moment, a fist came at me.

An explosion struck me and I was knocked onto my backside on the sand. Dancing lights distorted my vision and a droning hum swirled in my ears. I tried to come to my knees, but the pain muddled my senses and my movements became slower than normal.

He had punched me square in the face. I had no idea a mortal's strike could contain such force.

"Mind your own business," the larger man said, kicking a cloud of dust at me. I shielded my face and grunted as it scratched my eyes.

Another pair of footsteps approached—the other man, I assumed.

I could not see well through blurred vision induced by the impact and debris, but I tried hard to focus on them as they loomed over me. The man who had torn down my image was reaching past me to grab hold of the bag of grain.

"No!" I lunged to stop him, and at the same time, the other man drew back his arm, aiming for me again.

"Touch him and perish," a low, commanding voice boomed from nearby.

I could not see the new stranger's face as he bravely took a stand behind the man who had struck me. The sun peeked over his broad shoulders and blinded me with intense light.

"Who—?" the smaller man began to turn his head and ask. A loud thwack stunned him and he toppled on to his knees, instantly releasing his grip on the sack of grain.

I could see the stranger partly better now. His skin was the darkest and richest of all earthy tones. He wore a sleeveless crimson cloak that swept the ground near his feet and accentuated his muscular arms, which were as thick as pillars and as defined as the chiseled stone of Ra's statues.

He twirled a magnificent wooden staff deftly between his hands, as if it were a bolt of lightning he had mastered, and then faced his next opponent. Barely a breath passed between the first strike and the second as he swung his staff at break-neck speed and landed it on flesh, targeting the larger man this time. The sharp crack of bone made me cringe and a piercing howl of mortal pain had me covering my ears and squeezing my eyes closed.

How did a human move so swiftly? He wielded his staff with the speed of a storm.

"Let me help you," the voice spoke.

I opened my eyes and looked up at the man... or beast. Whatever he was. He was offering his arm out to me.

He had straight, glossy black hair that fell past his shoulders and unnaturally vivid eyes of the most dramatic shade of auburn. His long sharp face, with his strong nose and jaw line, exuded confidence.

I reached up and grasped his arm firmly so I could pull myself to my feet, but as I clasped onto him, it was as if he dragged me up with his strength alone, without any effort from me.

"Thank you for your help," I said, my voice breaking as I gazed down at the two unconscious men. "I... had not expected them to attack me."

His lips stretched into a wide, amused sort of grin. "You must learn to defend yourself, if you are to survive as a human," he said, raising an eyebrow. "Your things are there." He pointed behind me. I turned toward the grain and dates.

Human!?

"Wait!" I swerved back around... but the man had vanished.

I looked down. No footprints in the sand. No one nearby

to ask if—

"Aket?" I dragged my bags over to the tapestry vendor's table, set them on top, and knocked against the wood with my knuckles. "Aket?"

"Y-yes?" He poked his head up from behind the table.

"Did you see where that man with the red cloak went?"

"Who?" he asked, tickling his beard nervously.

"That man with the red cloak and the wooden staff. Where did he go?"

"I did not see him. I was..." He chuckled with embarrassment.

"Put your prized tapestry back up," I said, pointing behind the table. "The one of the falcon god."

"Yes, of course!" He scrambled around on the ground and finally came to his feet with the partially damaged piece in hand. "I will mend it first. It is in sorry condition and I do not wish to dishonor it."

"That is kind of you."

"Thank you for defending me," he said. "You are very brave and I will ask the gods to bless you for your courage."

He had not realized that it was not I who had taken out the thugs, but I would not tell him otherwise.

"Good day," I said, and then grabbed both bags off the table and headed back toward the Temple of Ra.

As I walked, I contemplated the intentions and identity of the dark warrior who had come to my aid. My face ached, but it would have been *much* worse, had he not arrived.

Friend or foe, he had risked a great deal to help me.

And... he had called me *human* as if he had known I was once something other than that...

18

I ARRIVED back at the temple with the bag of dates in one hand and the grain over my shoulder, clinging to my broken pride.

"I have done as you asked." I raised my voice so the wives would hear me from inside. The heavy sack plopped to the ground, but I held the dates.

Zahra poked her head out to see who it was and then approached me.

"Here," I muttered, looking to the side in hopes that she would not see my new wound.

"What happened to you!?" She reached up to grasp my face between her hands, and I flinched as her fingers pressed against the painful spot between my temple and cheek. She withdrew her hand and some blood colored her fingers. "Who did this to you?" She wiped her hand on her dress and then quickly looked over the rest of my exposed skin.

"I unwittingly started a fight in the marketplace. It will not happen again."

"Wait here." Zahra turned and walked over to a slab

near the entryway where a cloth and a large bowl of water had been placed. She dunked the cloth in the water and returned to where I stood, reaching up to pat the side of my face with the soft fabric.

"I feel like a child," I grumbled, trying not to cringe from her contact with the painfully swollen spot on my face. "I am so weak."

"You are human," she whispered. "Humans are frail and powerless at times. But we can also be strong. You must learn to find balance." She turned my face to the side and patted the spot one more time. "I apologize that this happened to you. I wish I could change things and give you back your powers so that I would not have to see you in pain."

I had been blaming myself for everything, but she showed unexpected remorse for the events, as well. None of this was her fault. *I* had broken the Oath; *I* had insisted on making her mine.

"I will make things right," I replied with a smile that sent a pinprick of pain up my face. "Do not blame yourself for my actions." I reached up to touch my face and my fingers drifted over the hot, swollen skin. Then they slid down over the coarse, prickly hairs budding from my chin. "This... Do you know how to get rid of this?" My face ached *and* itched.

Zahra raised an eyebrow at me. "Are the gods never required to shave?" she asked with a hint of jest.

"We appear as we like," I said, scowling. "And I do not like this hair."

She let out a quiet laugh. "Come with me. Bring the bags, please."

Zahra escorted me inside the temple and to the storehouse in the very back, which was tucked away past several other rooms and down a narrow hall. I did not know they had a storehouse full of preserved foods and supplies, but one could suppose the God's Wives sustained themselves throughout the year somehow.

She rummaged around on one of the shelves until she took hold of something and drew it out from behind a row of clay pots. It glistened in the low light and, as she lifted it up into view, I could see that it was a small, sharp blade.

"I have bled quite enough these last few days," I commented, glaring at the knife. "I do not wish to bleed by your hand, too."

"I can help you," she assured me. "I will not draw your blood with this."

How the crude thing might rid me of my frustrating facial hair was perplexing, but as long as it was wielded by her competent hands, I had no reason to fear it.

"Hold on to this, for now," she said.

I clasped it carefully, taking it by the copper handle, with the sharp edge pointed away from her. She moved closer and whispered, "There is a door down the hall behind you, adorned with a painting of a winged sun." She reached into a small slit in the side of her dress, by her waist, and withdrew a curved wooden stick with several small 'teeth' protruding from one end. "Take this key and enter the room. I will meet you there later this evening, after I have finished my duties. The windows will bring in light until dusk, but you may also use any lamps inside. Please try to be quiet, though."

"Will others come looking for me?" I asked.

"No. The room is only for my personal use and ceremonial preparations. No one will disturb you there. There is also a secret door and tunnel which will lead you to an exit outside the temple walls. I will show you that another time, for it is still too dangerous for you to wander."

"I did not know such things existed. The Temple of Ra contains many mysteries."

"We rarely speak of them," she said. "Now go. I am sorry I cannot help you more right now, but I will mix a salve for that bruise and assist you with the blade this evening."

"I will wait for you," I replied.

I turned and made my way down the hall with the wooden key in my hands. I followed a passageway aglow with candles until I came to a sharp turn and an entryway off to the side, out of view.

The double-door was short and narrow, and depicted the winged sun Zahra had described. The carvings were painted with bright colors and accented with polished gold and shards of rare, colorful stones. Near the middle of the doors, just below the sun, was a wooden box with a smaller peg of wood pushed through it. There was a hole on one side of the smaller peg. I slid in the wooden key with its pegs facing up and pressed it forward, wiggling it around until a click sounded. I pulled out the key and peg and the doors began to ease open toward me.

I entered, pulled the doors closed, and used the peg to lock them again from the inside; an identical lock had been placed there, too.

Sunlight poured in through small, rectangular windows

cut along the ceiling of the wall opposite the doors, lighting up the beautiful room and bringing life to the wall-to-wall murals surrounding me.

Colorful lotus flowers, geese, crocodiles, wild spotted cats, long-horned cattle... A very skilled artisan had painted the images with striking detail, knowing a prominent and sacred high priestess would gaze upon them at her leisure.

It was not a small room, nor a massive one, but it was more than spacious enough to provide an air of private luxury and comfort. In the center of the floor was a shallow, empty bath, built much like the pool at Isis' temple, except devoid of water.

A shelf full of jars and stored food stood on one side of the room, and on the other side was a long, carved cot with a matching gilded chair and table. Delicate white linens danced in the breeze as wind flitted through the windows overhead, and the extra ventilation made the room cooler than other areas of the temple.

I took a seat on the cot and pulled my feet up onto it. My muscles ached from my scuffle in the market earlier and my face was still inflamed and pulsing. I wondered if she had something for the pain in the row of jars and bottles on the shelf across the room, but I also knew that taking the wrong mixture of herbs could be fatal to a mortal body.

Sweeping illustrations of gods and goddesses decorated the ceiling, depicting many battles Ra faced during his ascension to king. I had heard of those battles, but now had begun to question the truth in them, as Ra was more tyrant than hero.

I leaned back on the bed and closed my eyes, wishing the

throbbing pain would fade. The soothing scent of incense drifted in from the other rooms of the temple, lulling me into a place of calm. Zahra would be back later, so I let go of all the things engaging my mind and drifted off to sleep.

I awoke to the gentle sound of bubbling water and sat up with a start, turning toward the pool in the center of the room. A stream flowed in from a series of channels around the perimeter of the pit. I stood and walked over to watch water proceed to fill the bath most of the way and then stop. I leaned over and dipped my fingers in. It was tepid and smelled clean—rainwater, most likely, though we had not had rain for several days. There must have been a cistern or aqueduct built into the roof or around the temple, which had stored the water. But who had turned on the mechanism that caused the pool to fill?

With the sun nearly set, the room had become aglow with fair azure light. I made haste to locate one of the lamps Zahra had mentioned, and then to find flint to light it. Now I could see that there were several other lamps around the room, too, so I quickly lit them all so as to save myself from being consumed by shadow.

Just as I sat back down, there was a knock on the door, and I froze, holding my breath as I listened.

Another knock, louder than the previous one.

I slowly approached the main entrance and waited.

"Horus?" It was Zahra.

I grabbed the key from nearby. The lock clicked and I drew out the wooden pin and opened the doors.

She bowed her head and passed by, carrying a tray of

food, drink, and medicines. I locked the door behind her. Seeing her made all my tiredness melt away.

"Will they come in search of you?" I asked, putting the key down beside the doors.

"No," she replied. "I told them that you left us, and that I would be here, cleansing myself of your presence."

"I see the pool has been filled." I gestured toward it.

"Yes. But not for me." She set her tray down on the table and moved a small off-white waxy cube to the side. She took a bowl and dipped it into the water to fill it halfway and then added in the waxy substance, agitating it until a layer of foam formed on top of the water.

"This place is meant to be a sacred cleansing room for use only by me during auspicious or troubling times," she continued. "But like with many things as of late, my opinions have changed, and I believe it will better serve you at this time."

The irony made me smile.

"The blade?" She lifted an open hand toward me.

I had left it beside the cot, so I quickly went to retrieve it.

"Here." I was careful to hand it over with the blade facing away from her fingers. She clasped it lightly and then motioned toward the bath.

"Would you..." She flourished her hand again and cleared her throat, gesturing for me to get into the water.

I approached the water's edge and looked down into the shallow pool; the bottom could easily be seen through the clear water, although grains of sand had settled on the floor, likely picked up along the way down the ducts leading inside the temple.

I removed my sandals and set them off to the side so they would stay dry. Next, I unwrapped the strip of fabric covering my snakebite and tossed it behind me. I was unsure about my tunic, but Zahra seemed to notice my fidgeting and said, "You may leave it on or remove it. Neither will cause me any discomfort."

Knowing she spoke the truth unabashedly, I untwisted the rope belt at my waist and pulled the tunic up over my head so that it would stay dry. Finally, I bent down and hopped in; the water barely came to my knees, but it was pleasantly cool and refreshing against my skin. As I sat and rested my back against the wall, Zahra came over and dumped an oily, black substance into the water. It dissolved quickly, swirling through as I swished my arm over it a few times. Then an intense smell infused the air. Smoky. Sweet. Earthy. I could not define it exactly.

"Myrrh quiets the body and mind," she announced, returning to her table to grab the bowl with the foamy layer on top. She knelt beside me and set it near my shoulders. "Can you turn your face toward me, please?"

I did as she requested and she scooped a layer of the watery white product from the bowl and slowly began painting it across my cheek and neck with her fingers. I did not understand what she was doing, but I also did not mind her warm touch and attention. After applying the foam, the glint of copper caught my eye and she brought the blade uncomfortably close to my face.

"Stay still, please," she said, holding the knife at an angle and barely touching the sharp edge to my skin. It made a coarse, scraping sound as she grazed it across my cheek, and I realized what she was doing.

"How does a woman know how to shave a man's face, when this man does not even know it, himself?" I asked, between strokes of her blade. She splashed water on my skin and applied more of the cream to my throat, chin, and just above my upper lip, continuing to work around the angles of my face.

"Press your lips together firmly," she instructed. The motion was foreign and strange, but I did as she asked and then she whisked away the hair from below my nose and chin. "I watched my father shave when I was a child," she finally answered my question. "I do not know how to do it well, but I am trying my best for you."

"You are *doing* your best," I said, "and I am thankful for it."

The magical thing she called myrrh was already beginning to soothe my sore muscles, so I closed my eyes and put my trust in Zahra's hands.

After several more moments of her painstakingly and ever so gingerly shearing the uncomfortable, budding whiskers from my face, she rinsed my skin with handfuls of water and asked me how it felt.

I lifted my fingertips to touch my chin; it was smooth again, but still not as smooth as it had been when I was a god. It would likely never feel that way again, and I would get used to it, with Zahra's help.

She swished the bowl around in the pool to clear the remaining soap and scooped fresh water into it. She poured it across my shoulders and then reached down to repeat the action.

"You are risking a lot to care for me," I said, running my damp fingers through my hair. The scent of myrrh had become less apparent now, but it lingered on my skin. "If you do not wish to have me in your life any longer, why would you take such a risk?"

She did not reply, so I shifted in the water and turned toward her, gazing up into her eyes. Her line of sight sunk toward my chest tattoo and she stared at it without speaking.

I came to my knees and climbed onto the edge of the pool, scooting closer to her so that I could reach up to tip her chin toward me. "What is it that occupies your thoughts right now?" I asked. "You have been so quiet, and yet, so attentive." My gaze followed her chin up to her pomegranate-stained lips, her small, sharp nose, and then to her endless brown eyes, which were suddenly avoiding me. I moved even closer to her, until my hip touched her knees where she knelt, and I reached my other hand up to stroke my fingers through her hair, over her ear, down toward her neck.

The beating of my heart picked up pace, until it resonated like a drum and I succumbed to an unfamiliar sense of nervousness. Strange, powerful desires began to grow in me, drawing me toward her as if we were two parts of a soul yearning to reconnect.

She cupped a hand on my cheek, pulled herself closer, and kissed me.

A breath caught in my lungs.

The heat of her skin pressed to mine was enchanting and warm—like no magic I had ever felt before. My hands slid to her back and I drew her in as her fingers combed through my hair and a thousand wonderful, tingling sensations made my entire body quake.

But then a heavy thought weighed upon me and I could no longer savor the moment.

"Zahra?" I did not want to break away from her kiss, but I had to ask a question.

She took a deep breath and smiled at me. "Yes?"

"I know you are sworn to your duties here, and that you have been hesitant to leave them before... but, if I swore to do everything possible to make a good life with you, would you become my wife?"

Zahra tilted her head.

She did not flinch nor scowl at my words, and instead let out a small laugh, which confused me greatly.

"I already have," she whispered, gazing at me with a look of admiration and contentment on her face.

"Y-you have? When?" I could only stare blankly, as I did not understand what she had meant.

She traced the tattoo on my chest. "Do you remember when you asked me to *become yours*?" she replied.

I nodded.

"I am a God's Wife, Horus, and you have proven to me that if any god deserves my loyalty, it should be you. You asked me to become yours, and I did."

"But... you said I was human now, and—"

"A wife does not abandon her husband once she has sworn herself to him, especially not when he is in most dire need of her support."

"And Ra?"

She tangled her hands together and shrugged. "I followed Ra blindly when I was a child because I was pressured to do so. I did not know any better, nor had I any other choice. You have sacrificed so much for me, and... if you would consider keeping a mortal woman as your wife, then I would consider starting a new life with you as my husband."

I raised a hand toward my heart. "The feelings burning in my chest right now," I started. "The racing of my heart is like... like a chariot of horses, their hooves pounding against sand. My breath... like a storm I cannot control. My mind is swirling. It is—"

"What I feel, too," she interrupted, her smile as sweet and beautiful as pure moonlight. She reached for my hand and brought it to her chest to press over her heart. The thump of each beat resonated through my fingertips.

"I do not understand it all," I added. "I have never felt so many things at once. What is this?"

"Passion. Desire. Love. It has many names."

"Love?" I cocked my head. "I have never *loved,* because gods are not obliged to. Do these feelings make sense to you, then? Are they... natural?"

"Yes. I think so," she said quietly, dropping her feet over the edge of the pool, into the water, and moving closer to me. Her fingers forked through my hair and our eyes met again. "Become mine, Horus," she whispered, the airy wisp of her voice charming my wits from me. "Become mine, and we will learn together."

19

ZAHRA drifted off to sleep in my arms.

As we lay together, a new sense of reason brewed within me. For a short while, I had forgotten what it was to be a god. Being human had its downsides—pain, weakness, mortality. But it also granted me the wondrous, inexplicable experience that is love.

Sensation.

Passion.

These did not exist in the realm of the gods.

Spending a single night with Zahra in my embrace—her body close to mine and her warmth reviving my sense of purpose—was enough to make me rethink the value of immortality.

And for a moment, I did not despise Ra for banishing me. For in his blindness and rage regarding my attempt to make Zahra my own, he rewarded me with profound emotions and a mortal body, allowing me to further consummate that desire.

I brushed my fingers through her hair and massaged

the back of her neck. She groaned softly in her sleep and nuzzled her face against me. The subtle pink undertone of her skin made her glow without makeup. I preferred her that way; her natural beauty was like a smooth river rock—shaped gently by time.

I could not sleep. Not with her there. Not even as perfect contentment coiled through me.

Too many questions wracked my mind.

It would be difficult, as a human, for me to keep her safe, but I would try my best. She had told me that we would discuss it the next day, but it troubled me now.

How would she survive without the village's offerings of food and supplies?

When would we leave? Where would we go?

With Egypt becoming the unfair target of Ra's wrath, I wondered if any place would truly be safe for us.

I closed my eyes and tried to rest, but each time I opened them, more light peeked in through the windows. It would be dawn soon, and I would have to let her go again.

My arms did not wish to. My heart ached at the thought of releasing her to the harsh world.

But then she stirred and her eyes eased open. "Horus?" She gazed at me sleepily and smiled. "I am happy you are still here."

"Why would I not be?"

"I thought, perhaps, last night was a dream." She brushed her fingers through my hair and scratched my neck playfully. "And that you would fade into a mirage once I awoke."

"No." I kissed her forehead. "I am no mirage. Not anymore."

She sat up and took a deep breath, reaching her arms over her head in a stretch. "Sadly, I must leave and prepare for the day."

I scooped up the red cloth from the floor and held it out to her. She offered me her wrist and I gently wrapped it around and tied it over the mark, letting my fingertips drift over the sensitive skin of her arm. She shuddered and pulled back, smiling coyly as she stood up from the bed.

"There is food in those containers," she said, pointing to the shelf. "You may have whatever you wish. I will try to bring you something else tonight."

"Thank you," I replied, taking to my feet. "I will do my best to think of a plan for us, meanwhile."

Before she could turn to leave, I took her by the hand and pulled her into a kiss.

"I must go," she said quietly, tugging away and smiling shyly.

I reluctantly followed her to the doors and opened them, being certain there were no wives near the storeroom or down the hall that would hear us. A wave of sorrow washed over me as she passed. Then I closed the doors behind her and listened as she locked it from the outside.

Following a small meal of honey beer bread, salted dried meat, and raisins, I was left with little more to busy myself than my own rampant thoughts.

As the sun ascended and light shone in, the temperature inside the room began to rise. I splashed water from the pool onto my face and dipped my feet into it for brief periods of time to relieve some discomfort.

After a few hours, I sat in the gilded chair by her table and looked up at the ceiling, scanning over the illustrations spanning from edge to edge. Strange heaviness filled my body and tightness squeezed my chest. The images became more difficult to focus on as they started to shift and blur.

A tingling shot through me and the hairs on my arms and the back of my neck started to perk up, making me shiver. The room became uncomfortable and, of all things, *cold.* I was compelled to stand, but a mysterious weight kept me seated. A burst of light illuminated the walls and the paintings faded.

He appeared before me—the tall, dark stranger who had rescued me in the marketplace, the long-haired man in the red cloak.

"You!?" I tried to stand again, but slid off the chair onto my knees, grimacing as my legs hit stone.

"Your father is in danger, Horus," he said, his deep, commanding voice filling the room with an uncanny, regal air. "You must come with me."

"My... father?" My lips hardly moved as my voice seemed trapped somewhere inside me. The influx of magical energy paralyzed my mortal body.

The man's dark, almost black eyes met mine and he pointed his staff at me. "We require your help," he said, more aggressively, and with a hint of beastly rumble to his words.

"W-who are you?" I strained to come to my feet, but an invisible force held me down.

"It has been some time... little brother," he replied. I lifted my head just enough to see a flash of red fire glint in his irises and the silhouette of a powerful black jackal's head appear over his human one.

Anubis, god of the underworld and guardian of the deceased.

"Stand, Brother!" he commanded. The powerful vibration of his words gave me a surge of strength and I was finally able to come to my feet.

But as I stood and scanned the room, all the walls faded to sand and we were swallowed up by transparent, shifting images of paintings no longer there. I glanced down and saw an outline of my human form lying sprawled across the floor.

"Your mortal body is safe while I am with you," Anubis spoke. "We stand in the rift now—the place between mortality and death. A place where time stands still."

His face transformed into his true animal form and fine, glossy black fur covered his body. As he tilted his head to look at me, the heavy, beaded wesekh around his neck and shoulders jingled. His thick, muscular arms were decorated with golden armbands and his skin covered in glowing, red tattoos of protective emblems. The tall, pointed ears, which oscillated slightly, listening in different directions, had been pierced with a single golden hoop earring at each tip.

Guardian of the underworld, assistant of Osiris, and guide to the souls of the dead, Anubis had to be one of the most foreboding and powerful gods I had ever seen.

And... he called me *brother!?*

Taller and stronger than me, our appearances were as different as night and day.

"Mortality has not been kind to you," he said with a

toothy, canine smirk.

"It has been well enough," I replied. "How is it that you are my brother?"

The underworld was a mysterious place, and although I was aware of Anubis' existence, I knew little about him.

"Though our mothers differ, we share the same father—Osiris," he replied. "He is in dire need of our help." Anubis bit down and snarled, revealing his long, jagged fangs. "Your exile made him weak with mourning, and as Osiris wept for the loss of a son, Set advanced upon the throne of the underworld."

"How?" I asked. While it clawed at me, I had no time to be angry with my father, or to pose questions about my estranged brother's origin.

"Like the coward he is, Set impaled our father in the back with his scepter, and then tore out his heart and plunged it into the River Nile."

"Is Osiris dead?"

"No. At least, not yet. Unbeknown to Set, Isis cast a powerful spell upon the body, binding his restless ka in place before it could part. But she cannot sustain the spell for long; it is draining her power swiftly. If we find and return the heart to Osiris' body, it is possible Isis can resurrect him and restore him to the throne."

"And if we cannot find the heart?"

Anubis lifted his head and sighed. "Then he will perish and forever be erased from this world."

I crossed my arms. "What has Ra to say about this atrocity?"

"The underworld is ours to govern as we see fit, but not

exempt from abiding by the Oath," the powerful jackal god growled. "Isis chose not to inform Ra because his past... *verdicts* were so poorly thought out. She has doubts about his competence and, since your exile, she is not alone in her opinions."

"But I am human now," I replied. "What can I possibly do to help the gods?"

My brother reached down to a leather bag hanging from the side of his gold chain belt and unclasped the metal snap on the flap. He reached his large hand inside and closed his fingers around something.

"As you may have suspected, there are still gods who are loyal to you," he said, removing his hand and unfurling his fingers before me. A small, amber-colored gemstone amulet shimmered in his palm.

"What is that?" I asked, afraid to accept it just yet.

"The divine Bastet grieves for you, and the benevolent cobra goddess, Wadjet, seeks revenge for Set's abuse of her precious form in his audacious attempt to kill you. I failed to protect our father. Together, we three have forged this talisman. It will not make you a god again, but it will grant you our protection and access to a significant portion of our magic, which you may use as you see fit to find the heart."

I reached out to take the amulet from his massive hand. The stone was deceptively lightweight, but the chain was heavy. "Why me?" I asked, staring at the mesmerizing golden-yellow stone as swirls of enchanted light danced through its facets.

"Only you, with your keen falcon sight, have the ability to search beyond the surface of the Nile for the heart."

I closed my fingers around the necklace and heaved a sigh.

"Your mother has faith in you, Horus," he added, reaching up to press his hand onto my shoulder and grin confidently.

My mother? Isis did not seem to care about my actions at all. Nor did I believe she had any faith in me or my abilities. It was Bastet alone who had warned me of my mistakes before it was too late.

"Please consider it, Brother," Anubis added; his deep red eyes gazed at me, and a hopeful smile of encouragement curled his canine muzzle. "If you help us, I will offer you assistance if Set retaliates."

"Retaliates!?" I sneered. "And what of my Zahra? How does she fit into this plan? Am I to leave her again?"

"Our father's life is of far greater importance than your feelings for a mortal."

"How dare you make naïve assumptions!" I shook my head and clenched the amulet tightly. "I have suffered enough at the hands of the gods. Brother, you have a loyal heart, and you mean well by coming to me for our father's sake, but I do not wish to be part of this."

"Very well." He lowered his head and frowned. "The decision is yours."

Another flash of bright light consumed me and I could no longer see my surroundings.

I awoke on the floor of Zahra's sacred room and came to my feet, sweeping sand from my arms and legs. Anubis had told me that time would not pass while I was there with him, so the day continued from when I had left it.

A whooshing noise and a wave of pressure zoomed through my head. I took a step, trying to stabilize myself, and my sandal bumped something, sending a tinny rattle across the floor. I glanced toward the noise and shuffled over to it.

The amber necklace Anubis had offered me lay upon stone, its crystal centerpiece flickering with energy.

I reached down to pick it up from the floor and examine it. The chain was finely made of pure gold, with thick, generously forged rings. The stone had many facets alive with fire, and its setting and bail had been etched with incantations of protective spells.

Did I want to help my father? Yes, of course. But did I want to sacrifice the new life I could have with Zahra as my wife in order to do it?

Never.

I clasped the necklace and walked over to sit in the gilded chair beside Zahra's table.

It did not sound as though my father had much time. What if I could not find his heart? What then? Would Osiris cease to exist? Would the future of the gods be changed altogether?

I balanced the necklace in my hand, rolling the stone back and forth over my fingers and watching light bounce from it.

"What do I do?" I spoke to the silent, empty room.

Sunlight changed hues outside and the light inside began to shift from gold to rich pink. I stood and lit several lamps around where I sat, so the room would not become too dark before Zahra's return.

Shortly after, there was a quiet rapping at the entrance,

a click, and then the doors opened. Zahra entered and I greeted her.

As she neared me, her attention fell to the necklace dangling in my hands.

"What is that?" she asked.

"Would you sit? I need to speak to you about something that is weighing on me heavily."

She nodded, and then walked over to the cot and sat on the edge. I joined her there and presented the amulet. "This was a gift from my brother, Anubis," I said, polishing the stone with my thumb.

"The guardian of the underworld is your—"

"It was news to me, as well." I cupped the necklace in my hands and gazed over at her. "My father, Osiris, is dying—his heart was torn out by his brother, Set, the god of chaos. My uncle, the same god who spoke against me at my trial." Zahra's brow wrinkled, but she continued to silently listen. "Anubis, Bastet, and Wadjet infused this stone with portions of their magic in an effort to allow me to return to the realm of the gods and attempt to save my father."

"Will you go?" she asked, worry glistening in her eyes.

"I do not know." I set the stone between us and reached for her hand. "I do not know how my actions will affect me, or if I will have the opportunity to regain my former status. Frankly, I am unsure if I want to."

"Why would you *not* want to be a god again?"

"Because I would lose you," I replied, brushing the backs of my fingers over her cheek. "I once thought immortality and power were all that mattered, but you have taught me otherwise."

"But if Osiris dies," Zahra whispered, contemplating her words, "what will happen to *us* when *we* die? If chaos reigns supreme in the underworld, will our souls wander for eternity without peace?"

"I do not know." I took a deep breath. "What should I do, Zahra? Risk life? Or death?"

She took my face into her warm hands and gazed affectionately at me. "Horus, I will be yours no matter what you decide, but I do believe that you should do what you can to help your father. The other gods have likely made great sacrifices to create that amulet. Do not forsake their generosity for *us*. We are but grains of sand in the oasis of time. This is about more than our souls; it concerns the souls of many generations." She took the necklace by the chain and lifted it. "I will love you no matter which path you choose, but you must choose the path you feel is right."

I glanced at the sparkling gemstone and then into Zahra's eyes.

"I will not let my father die," I said. "But I will also not renounce my wife." I tipped my head down. "I will use the power of my allies to rescue and avenge Osiris, and then I will find a way back to you. I swear it."

Zahra lifted the chain over my head and placed it around my neck.

A violent pulse of energy shot through me, forcing me to stand as a thunderous wave of light electrified my nerves. Warm, golden magic illuminated my skin from the inside out. My eyesight sharpened, my field of vision deepened, and I could see richer colors and details.

Then my face and arm tingled, and I looked down to

see the mark from the snakebite fade into my skin. Heat welled in my chest and I removed my tunic as my linen shendyt and golden jewelry manifested upon me once more.

"Your mark," Zahra said, staring at the tattoo on my chest.

I took a step toward the pool and looked down at my reflection. The tattoo flickered and the lines of the design danced upon my skin as if they were alive.

Light lived in me again, and although it did not change me back into a god, it filled me with fierce, impulsive energy, and I felt as strong as—if not stronger than—I was then. Gods were on my side, and with their combined magic, I would punish Set for his actions against the Oath, even if it meant breaking it again. There would be no greater reward than humanity by Zahra's side.

A brilliant ray of color swept across the room and Anubis appeared before us, his scarlet cloak rippling even though the wind was still. "Come, Brother," he said.

I approached Zahra and cupped her cheek with my hand. "I must go, but I will return." I leaned down to kiss her. "Have faith in me, my love," I whispered.

A bittersweet smile graced her lips. She released the knot from the red fabric on her wrist and removed it. The tattoo I had given her now glistened with the same radiance as my own, the shape shifting and resonating with renewed life. She lifted her wrist to her heart and pressed it to her chest. "Good luck."

Her passionate embrace and farewell kiss bestowed upon me the courage I needed to let go. I approached Anubis and he wielded his staff high overhead, weaving a spell that would take us away. I smiled back at Zahra as my brother and I disappeared from the earth.

20

LIGHT could not penetrate the inky-black canopy engulfing the underworld, where shadows surrounded us like wild dogs. Darkness impaired my vision, and my body felt weak and tingly as heavy, moist cold air congested my lungs. Anubis raised his staff and brought forth a blazing ball of fire which ignited the end and set our surroundings aglow with brilliant light.

I walked alongside him through the murky cavern until the painful sounds of a woman weeping slithered into my ears and discomfort ensnared me.

In a small alcove up ahead, Isis lay sprawled across a white marble floor, her face buried in her arms and tears of mourning glistening around her. Her wings were fanned out and the once radiant colored feathers had faded to somber, monochrome shades.

My father's body had been adorned with sacred amulets, laid out on a massive stone slab of polished basalt, and encapsulated in an eerie blue aura. His skin had drained of color, taken on a sickly shade of death, and his eyes gazed upward through lifeless, white haze.

I cleared my throat. "I have come to help find Father's heart." My words echoed.

Isis lifted her head and gasped. "Horus!? Oh, thank you!" She scrambled to her feet and came at me with open arms, but I avoided eye contact and looked to the side, denying her an embrace.

"I have come for the sake of the mortals," I continued flatly, "because my father's death would bring great tragedy to them—to those who pass and would have no king to guide them to the afterlife." My eyes met hers. "I swore to my wife that I would return to her when I am finished here. You must not try to stop me, Mother."

Isis' mouth eased open and she shook her head. "I would not interfere with your choices, my son." She placed her frail hands on my shoulders. A tattered grey feather fell from her wing to the floor. "You have already lost so much and yet you have still come to our aid. I am in your debt." She looked at Anubis. "*We* are in your debt."

"What do I do once I find the heart?" I asked, glancing at my father's body again—at the unsettling, inanimate form on display.

"Call for me," Anubis answered. "I will transport you back to the underworld and Isis will carry out the rest of the enchantment."

"But what of the Oath?" I asked. "It states we must not bring one back from the dead. Will you all be banished for this act?"

"We are righting what has been wronged," Anubis replied through gritted teeth. "If Ra threatens us for keeping *our* king alive, then we will rise against him, for we are no longer an army of one. Other gods will stand with us."

Brave, ambitious words came from his jackal mouth, and although I could not be part of such a rebellion, I, too, wished to see the vain Ra fall.

"I will search for the heart, and I will call for you when I have found it," I said.

Isis and my brother bowed toward me, and it was as if their faith sent a glint of fresh magic through my veins. But the sensation of warmth flitting across my skin must have been that of the amulet they had bestowed upon me, as I was no longer a true god.

Anubis raised his staff and pointed it forward. Light breached the darkness and a window to the outside world—to Earth—opened up before us.

I hesitated, at first, as it had been a few days since I had last flown through the sky like the falcon I once was. But when I glanced over at my brother, who donned a proud, confident smile, I felt stronger. If I could not trust the judge of the underworld with my soul, who could I trust?

I reached up and placed a hand near the opening, sticking my fingers through the surface, into the sooty grey clouds and vanishing violet horizon. The wind tickled my skin and implored me to take my place in the sky once more. There was no more time to waste on hesitation and afterthought.

I took a brisk step forward and plummeted through the doorway, tumbling through clouds and darkness as the sounds of night swallowed me whole and the songs of crickets and nocturnal beasts filled my ears. I shot toward the ground like an arrow and lifted my arms out to the sides to cling to a current and soar back up, narrowly avoiding an impact. Then I dove again, dragging a stream of cool air with me to help ease the sticky, dry heat that had blanketed the land.

In the distance, the River Nile twinkled with starlit ripples as the clouds and the moon shared a dance of light and shadow.

I swooped down toward the water and slowed my descent to carefully scan the riverbed for evidence of the hidden heart. I made several passes, following along the grand stretches and subtle curves, but nothing appeared out of place.

Rocks. Mud. Reeds. Birds nesting. Fish rested peacefully at the base of the river as I flew overhead and searched between every grain of sand with my acute vision. Then I narrowed my eyes and made a sharp turn downward, diving into the water.

I swam past lurking crocodiles and sleeping hippopotami, still turtles and resting frogs. My eyes scanned every nook and crevice, anywhere Set could have flung Osiris' heart.

But still, nothing.

I returned to the surface.

With a wave of my hand, I alerted the mighty crocodiles, interrupting their nighttime hunt. They thrashed about begrudgingly, until I manifested before them and their gazes locked on to me.

"I seek the heart of Osiris," I said, staring into the beady eyes of the toothy, rugged beasts. "Have you seen it?"

Their scaly faces lifted up through the water and, as a group, they shook their heads in one grand motion that made the marsh tremble. Surely the king of the underworld's heart would disrupt the living, should it be nearby, and yet the beasts knew nothing of it.

I dismissed them and carried on, making a third pass over the entirety of the river.

If I were Set, where would I have hidden my brother's heart?

In a place no one would think to look.

But where?

Set had always been jealous of my father's marriage to Isis, and that fact added an additional notch to the record of things he hated about Osiris.

I had lost little Nephiri to Isis' temple, either by a fatal accident or by Set's doing. Either way, my mother was rarely present there and the child's death had been utterly in vain.

What if my uncle had thought to bury it in that very place, knowing the sweet irony that Isis may never find it? Just as she had abandoned Nephiri that night, she would also not think to look for her husband's heart inside her own temple.

It was my belief that Set really was that wicked and conniving.

With instinct guiding me, I took off toward the Temple of Isis.

A nasty twinge made my stomach ache, and the thought of entering the place where I had discovered Nephiri's body filled me with guilt and regret. But I gathered my courage and flew through the entrance—straight down the narrow walkway, toward the massive statue of my mother sitting upon a throne. The lotus pond remained unclean and littered with decay. I gazed up at my mother's stone face and sickness roiled in me. Thick tears of blood oozed from her eyes, pooling in her lap.

I was right. Death and chaos had occupied the once sacred place, and a vile curse was in motion, likely set forth by my uncle.

Paint chipped and crackled from the carvings on the ceilings and walls, leaving flecks of color at my feet. Wisps of black shadow—the most dangerous of all darkness—drifted up from the pools surrounding me. The walls pulsated with sadness and pain, and a pervasive sound resonated from the statue of Isis. Each step closer amplified the vibrations, until my head pounded and it became difficult to stay focused with so much noise assaulting me.

I dropped to my knees at her feet and held my aching head, the pain more potent than a mortal wound.

I had to stand!

I had to gather the strength to find my father's heart.

So I pushed up from the floor and reached toward her hands, which rested upon a lap covered with blood. A thunderous rhythm shook the room and the onslaught of negative energy made my vision hazy, forcing tears of red to fall down my cheeks, tinting my vision with scarlet and stinging the surface of my skin.

Through blood and stone, I spotted a vein of indigo light up ahead—a spell cast to shroud the heart!

"Forgive me, Mother." I pried the nearest brick from the edge of the pond, hissing as a curl of shadow-smoke pricked my hand. My arm drew back and I smashed the brick against the statue, inflicting a violent crack on the leg, which stretched toward her torso.

The statue shifted, as if it had come alive, and let out a howl of pain, sending me staggering back a half step.

Mother!?

No.

I could not let Set's trickery fool me. It was a cursed statue and not the real Isis.

The sound pierced my ears and I screamed in agony, clutching to the stone in my hands as I pulled back and struck the statue again as hard as my muscles allowed. She cried out a second time and I grimaced.

Now that a large fracture had been made, I threw the stone off to the side and wiped blood from my face so I could see clearly again.

The throbbing of the heart became louder and louder as I drew nearer to the jagged rift in the statue. There, past rigid edges, beyond the indigo light and deep down inside the chasm of shattered stone, was Osiris' heart, pulsing.

The shadow-smoke serpents began to rise up from the pond, creeping onto the pathway and spiraling toward me. I reached inside the crack and stretched my arm as far as I could to try to grasp the throbbing heart.

Liquid fire sliced through my ankle, and I jolted as a coil of smoke wrapped around my leg.

The heart was in my fingers now, and I had to retain my grasp as I carefully worked to free it from the statue. I planted my feet and pulled back, dragging the impossibly heavy organ out, biting down as blackness singed my flesh.

"Anubis!" I grunted, cringing as shadow-smoke struck at my exposed skin.

The heart was nearly clear of the statue now and my amulet beamed with golden light.

A flash filled the room and Anubis appeared beside me.

"Brother!" He clasped a large hand onto my shoulder and the heart suddenly felt lighter. I fell back against him, clutching my father's heart with both hands. He swung his staff toward the smoke and it withdrew, shriveling back into the pool.

"You can fight shadows?" I asked, trying to catch my breath and stand straight. The horrible black wisps were angrily lashing out from the distance, but unable to reach me anymore.

"Normally, yes," Anubis replied. "But my powers have weakened, since sharing them with you."

The floor shook and I stumbled, grabbing onto the statue's remains to keep myself from falling. The heart was still pressed to my chest with my other hand.

"The temple is collapsing!" Anubis shouted. "We must leave at once." He took one final swing at the serpentine smoke creatures and then lifted his staff up high. A blast of light engulfed us and we were transported back to the underworld.

My eyes slowly adjusted as Anubis lit his staff aflame to light the way.

After my hearing had been battered by so many sounds in the temple, the silence was unnerving. A residual pulsing sensation rattled my thoughts, but softened as moments passed.

"Give me the heart!" Isis wailed, crawling over to me from her place at the foot of Osiris' deathbed.

'No,' was my first thought, though I did not understand

why.

I brought the thumping thing close to my chest and clutched it possessively. I had risked too much to simply hand it over without hesitation.

"You cannot bring him back on your own, Horus," Anubis spoke.

My body shook with anxiety and fear, and I succumbed to an unfamiliar wave of thoughts seizing my mind. "If my father dies, who will take his throne?" I asked.

"What do you mean?" Anubis replied, tilting his head and narrowing his eyes. "*Set* is trying to take it from us *all*."

"That is not what I asked," I said. "Who is the heir to the throne of the underworld!? You? Or me?"

Anubis looked back at me with a mix of confusion and anger crinkling his brow.

"You are," Isis cried, coming to her feet. "You are the rightful heir to the throne, Horus, but why do you ask?" She reached toward me. "Please, give me the heart so that I may save your father."

"Give it to her!" Anubis roared, and took a step closer to me, threatening me with the tip of his emblazoned staff.

The accusations rising to my lips were discomforting and unbecoming of me. I tried to disregard them, but...

"If Osiris dies," I began, grasping the heart tightly, almost as if I may crush it between my hands, "and *I* assume the throne, will I become a god again? Will I regain my powers... *and* acquire his?"

"The shadows have poisoned him," Anubis said to Isis. Then he turned to me. "You must fight the shadow-smoke's influence."

"No," I objected. "You want the throne for yourself."

No! What was I saying? I did not want the throne of the underworld!

All I wanted was...

I could not remember what I had wanted.

"It is Set who commands the shadow beasts' venom!" Anubis growled. "Horus, if you destroy the heart, Set will destroy you and we will lose the throne forever. You are mortal now and you thrive on borrowed magic! Come to your senses, Brother! Fight the darkness!"

The heart continued to beat in my grasp. The sound was reminiscent of... something.

"Remember your wife!" Isis said. "If you exchange mortality for the throne of the underworld, you will never see Zahra again."

Zahra?

I shook my head and tried to rid my mind of the black haze.

The heartbeat reminded me of someone, Zahra, and how I had listened to her heart pulsing quietly in the night as she lay beside me.

No. I did not wish to be the ruler of the underworld. The shadows had tainted my thoughts.

"Please give us the heart," Isis called again.

I wanted to save my father. I wanted to save Osiris.

"Here." I passed it to Isis, who caught it with great care.

The darkness released me, replacing my clouded thoughts with terrifying clarity and truth, revealing the consequences of my actions—I had nearly let my father die.

"I am sorry," I apologized, and then approached my

mother beside Osiris' body. "How might I help?"

In the center of my father's chest was a gaping hole, festering and bubbling with strands of putrid flesh.

Anubis came around the other side of the slab and lifted his staff high overhead. "Place the heart over the wound," he instructed.

I rested my hands over my mother's and, together, we lowered the organ down toward the hole. My brother began to speak in a foreign tongue, and although I could not understand his words, each one from his mouth made the heart pump a little faster.

Then my mother released the heart and it began to sink into the wound. She, too, burst into a hymn, singing in the same unrecognizable language.

I knew nothing of the ways of the underworld gods, and I felt helpless during the ritual. But it *was* working, and that was all that mattered.

Strands of torn flesh took on their own life and enveloped the heart like roots of a tree, drawing it slowly inside his chest cavity and then stitching together the wound until only a patch of discolored flesh remained.

We all stood in silence, staring at the body, hoping for something to happen. But my father did not move, or speak, or blink.

"He will live," Isis said, clasping his hand between hers. I could still hear the heart beating, though it resonated from inside him now.

"Are you sure?" I asked. I could not imagine how his pale, cadaverous flesh served as an indication of anything more than death.

"He must be embalmed to preserve what is left of his body," Anubis announced. "Only then will she be able to complete the spell and imbue the breath of life back into him."

"Then will he live?"

"Yes. In a sense," Isis declared. "He will be well enough to resume his place as king of the underworld, but he will not be all he once was. Still, a partial life is better than death."

"Perhaps," I said with a shrug, though I did not wish to return to Zahra "partially alive."

21

ANUBIS twirled his staff and a bolt of flame coiled around it, igniting the entire length with streams of citrine and amethyst fire. One end exploded and a black blade burst from the tip, transforming the weapon into a spear.

"Take this." He offered it out to me. "The Staff of Justice will guide you through the darkness and give you the power to confront and defeat Set."

"*Defeat* him?" I scowled. "Why must I confront him at all? I am still mortal and I have much to lose."

"Bastet, Wadjet, and I have all sacrificed a portion of our own magic in order to forge that amulet and bring you here. In doing so, we have all been weakened and cannot possibly challenge him on our own or together. Not with the same strength you have now. We will protect you as best we can, and it is our belief that you will triumph, as justice always shall." He stretched his arm out and offered me the staff again. "Take it."

I wrapped my fingers around the cold metal spear and he released it into my grasp. As it tipped forward, the heavy thing nearly pulled me over, and I struggled to catch my balance and hold it straight. Anubis was the embodiment of a seasoned, battle-born warrior, and although I was not, some part of me was eager to embrace the idea of becoming one.

I lifted the staff with both hands, straining, at first, until it abruptly shortened in length and became substantially lighter—as if it were adjusting to serve me better. A buzzing sensation tickled my fingers and a wave of energy rushed through my hands, up my arms, and toward my brain, entangling with my memories and implanting skills there which I had never learned. The borrowed knowledge filled me with newfound confidence in my ability to wield the blade.

Anubis grinned, his pointy teeth glistening. "How does it feel now?"

I juggled it between hands and then swung it forward in a practice strike. The movement felt surprisingly fluid and natural. "It is *much* more manageable. Thank you."

"Wield it against your enemies, and it will serve you well," Anubis said. "Wadjet awaits you on the surface. She will take you to Set."

I tipped my head toward my mother, who was deep in concentration, orchestrating a daunting spell on my father's body. "Goodbye."

She did not look up or reply.

"I am ready, Anubis."

My brother smirked and pointed at me. "*You* have the staff now."

He was right.

I raised it above my head and a gush of energy spun

through me, racing down toward my fingers and into the staff. The room flashed, and I found myself in a dark oasis somewhere on Earth.

A soft hissing sound caught my attention; a small, delicate leaf-green cobra slithered toward me. It halted at my feet and stared up at me with rich grassy eyes, flicking a pale pink tongue at the air.

I sensed great magic exuding from the creature and I bent down to offer a hand out to her, which she then used to coil up and entwine herself around my forearm.

"Ssset must pay for exploiting my children and my image," she whispered in a pleasant, feminine voice, unveiling her vibrant red and gold hood as anger flushed through her serpentine body. "I will take you to Set's throne room—a place of molten fire and pestilence set in a barren wasteland in Upper Egypt. You must defeat the malevolent fiend and claim his land. Only then will we be free of his tyranny and deception."

Claim his land?

"But what about the Oath?" I asked, gazing into her elegant cobra eyes. "Each of you who stands against Set stands against Ra, and I will not lose my life for this act, not when I have a wife to return to and a reason to stay alive."

Wadjet gracefully slid up my arm, her smooth scales like water across my skin, and uncoiled her tail to use it to tap the glowing amber necklace hanging above my tattoo.

"Thisss is a gift from us all. You have our protection, Horus. We will not let you die. Set has broken the Oath numerous times, and if Ra continues to turn a blind eye and not deal punishment for the deeds he has done, then we will. Do not forget, Horus." She glided over the back of my neck and let her tail hang down on one side. "You bear the mark of your destiny."

The outline of my tattoo remained aglow with warm light, and I was reminded that Wadjet was depicted there upon my chest.

"I will guide you," she said, and then slithered down my other arm, onto Anubis' staff, where she twisted her body around it tightly, clinging below the blade.

"Very well," I replied, bracing myself.

We vanished from the oasis and reappeared in a desert, encircled by massive braziers burning beneath a blackened sky. I looked up, but could not see a single star, as thick dark cloud cover drifted overhead.

Wadjet's eyes glittered like emerald beacons as she scanned our surroundings and twitched her tail. I walked across stone and sand, my sandals crunching weathered bone fragments and shards of crumbling limestone. I did not see a throne, nor did I see Set.

"He is not here," I said in a hushed tone, gazing past a tall iron cage full of blazing coals; flames danced violently in the dead breeze, reaching up high and threatening to climb over and spill across the ground.

"He is here," she hissed. "I feel him. He is hiding."

The moment the words reached my ears, a faint rustle sounded behind me and I went tumbling headfirst toward the ground, knocked forward by a heavy blow to the back.

Anubis' staff flew out of my hands and Wadjet uncurled herself and leapt to safety.

A low, gravelly growl came up behind me and I twisted

around.

No one was there.

"What are you doing on *my* land, Nephew?" Set's distinct voice sounded. He remained invisible.

I bolted out of the way—too slow—and was struck in the side, this time with dark energy that resembled the bite of the shadow serpents from Isis' temple.

"Retrieve the staff!" Wadjet cried, her eyeshine signaling her location. I scrambled to my feet and lunged after it.

"Show yourself, coward!" I clasped onto the staff and my jaw tightened as I searched for movement. Set had been known to use trickery, not bravery, to win his battles, and I would not be fooled by such antics.

Midnight darkness impaired my vision, and I had to use light cast by the distant braziers around us to detect distortions or footprints in the sand. I willed the staff to become a torch; a fury of colorful purple flames danced, bending strangely in one direction, as if being pulled toward something. A plume of shadow energy brushed against me and I veered around, swinging the staff faster than I knew I could, landing a swift blow.

Set yelped in pain and became visible, clutching his face. Then his image began to fade as he attempted to vanish again. Wadjet darted across the sand, coiled up his leg, and twisted herself around him, forcing him onto his knees and disrupting his spell.

"Hurry!" she said. "I cannot restrain him for long."

"You attempted to kill your brother, Set!" I snarled, seething as I approached him. My hands tightened around the staff. "You dare claim that my actions are unfit for a god, when you, yourself, do not deserve to be one!?"

Set cowered before me, his shaking, wrinkly hands rising to clasp together near his chest. His piercing yellow eyes glistened in the firelight and his misshapen face struggled to convey remorse.

"I did what had to be done to uphold the Oath," he said, his crackly voice wavering. "I do what Lord Ra asks of me, but I am helpless without his support, and I have little to show for all my labor. I may rule Upper Egypt, but I have few followers. That is why I go through such great lengths to maintain this accursed thing." He shrugged his shoulders, indicating he had meant his cloak of souls.

Was he jealous of me, then?

Jealously was no reason to commit murder.

"You *would* have followers if you were just and kind," I replied. "Like many other gods."

"But I am ugly and weak," he moaned, crumbling over and placing his hands upon the sand. His sparkling cloak pooled at his feet. "And my body is old. It does not treat me well. In a lapse of judgment, I vainly believed the underworld might suit me better. That, perhaps, I could do some good there, which I could not do here in *this* desolate place."

Wadjet's grasp on him loosened and she peered up at me as though she did not know what to do.

It was true that Set was a frail god, and that his malnourished body and mutilated ears made him appear revolting to some, but I would not pity his poor choices. He could have lived with the other gods in the palace, but he *chose* to forgo that for this fiery wasteland. It was not forced upon him.

"You, Horus," he continued, his face still turned to the ground, "are young and vibrant, while I am bent with age and feebleness."

Set *was* a very old god.

"That mark," he said, lifting his gaze toward me and pointing unsteadily to my chest. "It means that you are destined to be greater than Ra, you know? We are not so different, you and I."

I *did*, at one time, wish to be greater than our king, to overthrow him and rule in his place as the living sun. But—

"Immortality is not everything, Uncle," I replied. "Not anymore."

"Oh?" He tried very hard to smile, but it was only a weak crinkle in his curved snout. "Would you tell me more? How did mortality change you into such a wise god?" He gazed eagerly at me and tilted his head, bringing a hand toward his ear as if he had wished for me to move down closer. "Tell me, please. I will listen, Horus, but my hearing is not as it once was."

I did not understand his change of heart; it bewildered me.

I took a step back and turned away, trying to hide my uncertainty.

Did he really want to know why I had changed?

What could my ancient uncle possibly learn from my meager experiences in the human realm?

"Horus!" Wadjet's voice cut through the night and I turned toward Set again.

He had come to his feet, his arm was drawn back, and—

Obsidian claws slashed across my face, tearing my sight

away. I bent over and screamed in pain as magical energy poured from my eye socket, streams of golden light sifting through my fingers and dissolving into the sand.

"How dare you consider yourself a god!" he jeered. "You. Are. Weak."

I covered my wounded eye tightly with one hand and tried to focus on him with my other. I was lucky he had only hit one, but the amulet's magic was being siphoned away from me through my wound and I could not stop it. At this rate, I would lose my brother's, Wadjet's, and Bastet's magic in a fleeting breath.

My fragile human hand could not keep the power inside me and it continued to squeeze through my fingers.

"You should have stayed with your mortal woman," Set spoke. "I may have let you live, as I do not care for the priestesses of Ra. But you had to return to avenge your father. You should have let me take his throne, and then you could have been *happy* with your insignificant mortal."

Zahra was *anything* but insignificant.

And I had promised to return to her.

I would not let Set, Ra, or anyone else stop me from keeping that promise.

"Please, Uncle," I spoke quietly, mustering the strength to push through the pain, while pretending to cower at his feet, just as he had at mine. "Spare me, for I am ignorant and you are ancient and wise."

"What are you doing, Horus!?" Wadjet hissed and slithered beneath me to look up at my face.

"The staff," I mouthed to her, my head still turned down where Set could not see my expression.

"You may be young and ignorant," Set continued, "but at least you are wise enough to admit your mistakes."

The magic oozing from my eye continued to color the ground with flecks of bright flickering light, and it provided cover for Wadjet to grasp onto the staff with her tail and wriggle it closer to me without Set's knowledge.

"Perhaps, I may have some use for you," Set said, turning partially away as he scratched his jaw. "*If* you bow to me."

His black and red cloak twinkled with the lost souls he had harvested for his own foul deeds. I would not become one of them, and I would not subject Zahra to his cruelty by allowing him to go free.

I reached across the sand, seized the staff, and used it to propel myself to my feet. A blaze of orange fire erupted from the blade and I swung it at Set, slicing into the cloak. The fabric split at his shoulders and fell into a heap upon the ground. The vibrant threads of lost souls dissolved across the sand like feral glow worms burrowing to escape.

"No!" he croaked, scrambling to scoop up and clutch the fading fibers as they drained through his fingers.

His eyes became dull and hazy and the color of his skin even greyer than before. "What have you done to me!?"

Set's cloak of captured kas was the source of his power, and now that it had been destroyed, his skin turned dusty and crackled with age, and his once potent aura withered.

"You will harm no one else," I slurred and huffed a labored breath. Pain from the magic spilling from my mortal body made me quake. Wadjet twisted up the staff again and her presence imbued me with the willpower to carry on.

My knuckles paled as I squeezed the spear with all my might. I was compelled to bring back my arm and strike again, this time, to vanquish him from my life... to punish him for all the evil he had done and all the vile things he had intended to do.

But I would not lower myself to becoming a murderer, too.

I would *not* deliberately kill another.

"If you hold such contempt against the *insignificant* humans who make up our world, then I challenge you to survive amongst them. May you begin your journey in the treacherous darkness you revere." I grunted and pointed the staff at him. He staggered back. A window to another place opened behind him. Wadjet twirled down the spear and crawled up behind his leg, where she nipped him in the shin and sent him stumbling through the doorway.

I would not kill Set, but he would face the unforgiving desert on his own—the place where he could harm no other.

Searing pain shredded through me again and I fell to my knees and shuddered, clutching my wounded eye.

"Let me help you," Wadjet whispered. She slithered closer and raised her head high.

"What more can you do?" I asked, barely able to focus on her scaly face with only one viable eye.

She did not reply, but the edges of her serpent mouth stretched into a gentle, reptilian smile and her emerald irises shimmered.

A warm, tingling sensation washed over my face and intense heat welled in my eye socket. Prickling sharp pains rushed through me and I doubled over and squeezed my eyes shut, gasping for breath.

Slowly, the sensation began to diminish and the heat cooled.

I eased my eyes open.

The colors around me had become altered. I looked down at Wadjet, who donned a sweet smile, and noticed one of her eyes had changed into a glossy onyx orb. My vision was as sharp as pure falcon sight, but now I was gazing through one eye of a bird and one of a snake.

As I opened my mouth to speak, she flicked her tongue at me and shook her head. "Do not thank me, Horus," she said, and then coiled into a tight circle and vanished into a plume of green fire.

Wadjet had given me one of her eyes.

But she had asked for nothing in return.

Set. Set was gone, was he not?

My mind spun with so many thoughts, I could barely keep them straight.

Zahra! I could return to her and...

No. I had to speak with Ra first.

Was I a god now? I could not have been. Not with such intense pain tearing through me. But I was not a mortal, either, or else Wadjet's eye would not have taken to me.

Perhaps I was neither.

I came to my feet with the staff in hand and gazed down at the amber necklace the gods had made for me. It had gone dull and opaque. The gemstone no longer sparkled with light. Was it empty? I did not know, but Bastet could advise me.

I envisioned myself at her side in the Palace of the Gods,

and the staff transported me to her room in an instant.

In the long garden corridor which was part of her chamber, it was quieter and darker than usual. Bastet's lair was typically filled with singing birds dashing between the canopy of trees making up her ceiling, along with beautiful spotted wildcats playfully chasing bugs about. There was usually an abundance of life and joy in the place, but right now, it was dark and still.

I walked through the room, passing beneath brittle dead branches and stepping through dried leaves and yellow grass, until I saw her, facing away from me on a small bench up ahead. Several cats curled up quietly at her feet. Not purring. Not sleeping. Just waiting beside her in silence.

I gazed toward the ceiling and screened the gnarled branches sprawling overhead. Not a bird in sight.

"Bastet?" I approached her slowly. One of the cats looked up at me. "Bastet?" I repeated, placing a hand onto her shoulder. It felt unusually boney. "My friend?"

She turned to face me and I stopped breathing. We stared at each other, and the deep sadness in her faded eyes made my heart ache and my stomach churn.

Bastet's face had become thin and frail, narrow and pointed—the fur on her muzzle now short and dark, and her ears very small and sharp. The dense coat that once accented her lean muscles had vanished and her body had wilted into that of a dainty black cat's.

"I am glad you are alive," she uttered, and then gazed back down at her thin paws and cupped them in her lap.

"W-what happened?" I stammered, barely able to quiet

my hastening breaths.

"Ra punished me for helping you," she said, her voice so quiet and broken that I could scarcely hear her. "But I did not argue with his accusations, for they were true."

Her support had cost her her beautiful lioness face and he had forced upon her that of a simple house cat, in return.

Punishing and banishing *me* for my disobedience was one matter, but for Ra to steal away the innocent face of my beloved friend was cruel and unforgivable.

I laid the staff down at my feet and then raised my arms and wrapped them around her narrow shoulders, hugging her tightly.

"Thank you for all that you have done for me, my friend," I said. "Ra may command the sun, but I now command knowledge of compassion and love. Only I understand how significant mortal faith can be and what loyalty means."

She raised her head again and I released her to stroke my fingers across her sleek brow.

"You have Wadjet's eye?" she asked, gazing at it and then at my tattoo. "Then the mark is true. The cobra goddess is but one of many who will assist you in your journey."

"Set is gone," I said quietly.

"Gone?" Her ears perked up and faced me. "Is he?"

"I did not kill him, if that concerns you, but I have mercifully allowed him to experience mortality on his own."

A fleeting smile curled a corner of her lips.

"The wheels of destiny have been put in motion," she said. "Confront Ra and speak the truth of what you have seen. Inform the gods about the perils you have faced and vanquished, and of the vile deeds of your uncle and his king."

She clasped my hand in her delicate cat paws. "You have my faith, Horus. Now and always."

22

A SURGE of emotions rushed through me: anxiety, anger, fear, passion. Emotions I could not fully comprehend before I had been turned mortal, and they compelled me to challenge Ra's authority as the all-knowing, all-righteous king he claimed to be. I wanted him to acknowledge that I had matured and learned from my mistakes. But most of all, I wanted—*needed*—him to realize that becoming human was not a punishment, and that he could not control who I loved or condemn those who had shown kindness toward me.

I arrived at the main garden courtyard, to the place where Ra had handed me a broken amulet, crippling my powers from the start—the place where I had been made to look like a fool in front of my peers.

I entered through the stone archway and the memory of that fateful day made my heart race and discomfort squeeze my stomach. It would seem that he had been expecting me. Ra sat upon his stately throne in the circular courtyard, surrounded by the other gods. The seats directly beside him were empty, with neither Isis, nor Bastet present.

The cauldron of souls in the center of the room burned brighter than it had in centuries, and it intimidated me. It raged with the imprisoned kas of Ra's defeated adversaries, and I tried to convince myself that my own would not join them.

I wanted to believe the other gods were happy to see my return, but it did not appear that way; their vacant expressions were impossible to read.

Already, it felt like another trial.

"Horus," Ra addressed me, lifting a hand from his armrest. "You have found your way back."

"With no help from you," I retorted, struggling to keep myself calm as fury began to kindle in me.

"Have you come to beg for forgiveness?" he asked, stroking his chin.

"No." I shook my head and tightened my grasp on the spear.

His eyes locked onto it and his brow wrinkled angrily. "You dare to bring a weapon into this sacred place?"

"Ironic," I replied, "that you would call the Staff of Justice—a gift given to me by the guardian of the underworld, my brother, Anubis—a weapon. I should think you would recognize one of your kingdom's prized relics."

I approached the throne, glancing over the array of animal-headed gods around me, and stood, planting the staff firmly on the ground at my side. The metal made a satisfying clink against the stone floor.

"Then why have you returned?" Ra asked.

"Set tried to murder Osiris and steal the throne of the underworld."

A loud gasp rang through the crowd.

Ra forcefully pushed up from the throne and stood. "How dare you step into my courtyard and make profane accusations against my personal advisor."

"See for yourself," I said, pointing to Wadjet's sacred eye. "Set tore out my father's heart, and then took my eye as a trophy when I confronted him. Had it not been for the goddess, Wadjet, I would be half blind or worse. You stripped me of my defenses, rendering me vulnerable to death."

"I made you mortal," Ra said, scowling. "I punished you for seducing one of my disciples, and now you come here to confess that you attacked my royal advisor? I should dispose of you, but the Oath forbids it."

"Are you admitting that I intimidate you, then?" I met eyes with several of the gods as I gazed over the crowd. "As a petty human?"

Low chatter began to resonate around me.

"Quiet!" Ra commanded, raising his arms into the air. He took a step forward. "Horus, you were a young and inexperienced god when I restricted your magic, and now you are no god at all. And yet, you have the audacity to come here with borrowed power to make obscene accusations!? What have you done to Set? He did not attend when summoned." His brow sloped sharply and he narrowed his eyes. "Did you murder him, too?"

"I did not murder my uncle." I rolled my shoulders back and took a deep breath. "I granted him the very same mercy you did to me."

His eyes widened. "You made him mortal!? How!?"

"The method is unimportant," I countered. "What *is*

important is that he tried to kill me and nearly killed my father, too. I did what had to be done in order to stop him."

"Without my permission!? Who do you think you are?"

"I *think*..." I cleared my throat. "I *know* I am the heir to Osiris' throne. It would serve you well to have patient ears in my presence."

"My sentence was final," he continued. "Those who have brought you here will pay for their betrayal."

"They did not *betray* you," I corrected. "Wadjet sacrificed an eye in order to save my life."

Ra squinted and twitched angrily.

"The brave and honorable Bastet spent centuries serving as your faithful, unyielding guardian, and you punished her without hesitation."

"She aided an exile!" Ra snarled.

"Because she knew, in her heart, that your blind eye toward Set's actions and your brutal judgment toward me was unjust."

Ra's eyes were aglow with fire and the seed of intimidation took root in me, making my hands sweat and my heart thump against my ribs.

I grappled my thoughts, trying to put them into efficient, convincing words. What could I say to prove Ra no longer deserved his position as king of the gods? What could I do to illustrate that I had learned more about the mortal realm from being immersed in it briefly, than he had in the centuries spent watching from the sky?

The mortal hardships I had faced taught me to value life and the nuances of human emotion. They gave me the ability to feel what no god had ever been able to feel before.

Then a question rose to my lips.

One I *knew* he could never answer.

"Can you describe pain?" I spoke up.

"Pain!?" Ra scoffed and looked around as if he had thought I had asked him the question in jest.

"Yes," I replied calmly. "Describe pain so that your court of gods may understand it better."

"Gods do not feel pain," he answered.

"How about hunger or sickness? Joy? Love? Passion? Can you describe those, then? Pick any one of them." I shrugged and tipped my head toward him. "You are King of the Gods, after all. And, at the very least, you should comprehend the very primitive components of the humans you oversee. For it is only because of their faith in us, that we have any power at all. Their temples and their prayers keep us strong. I have witnessed this firsthand."

The crowd gasped again and Ra looked around, startled by the reaction.

"Hush!" He raised his hands. "All of you, quiet!" Ra stomped down the small flight of stairs leading to where I stood. "I do not need to explain such pettiness in order to rule effectively." His fiery eyes glared at me. "Humans are but sheep, and we are the shepherds who drive them. We do not need to know how they fe—"

"Like a blade piercing flesh," I interrupted, "the skin splits, tearing open a void that exposes your raw, vulnerable nature. It causes your teeth to clench, the coarse grinding sound twisting into your brain, while your fingers curl into tight, uncomfortable fists involuntarily. The sensation pushes you to your knees, because you cannot withstand the sharp spark that bites at your skin, singeing the flesh until it sickens the veins and they vomit blood—your precious lifeforce. You watch, helplessly, as it pours from your body, all while dangerous venom infiltrates your nerves and lights you on fire from the inside, and you cannot cast a spell to stop it, because you are a frail human. That was the bite of the serpent Set forced upon me after I became mortal. *That* is pain, and a very minor assessment of it, at that."

"I did not order Set to harm you," Ra defended.

"Nor did you prevent him from doing so." I narrowed my eyes.

A flush of heat swept through me and I felt my magic growing stronger. I glanced around the room and noticed many of the gods were staring with awe and captivation, as if they were hanging on my every word. The feeling indicated that their faith was affecting me in some way.

"But pain is only a grain of sand in the spectrum of mortal emotions," I added.

"Are they all so grand and terrible?" mighty Sobek asked, speaking up from the crowd in his gruff, crocodile voice.

Ra pressed his lips thin and his nostrils flared. As he turned to gaze back at me, the fire in his irises had dimmed, fading to a placid rose. The change did not appear to be purposeful, however, as his face still wrinkled with contempt.

"Grand, yes, but not all are so terrible," I replied, glancing back at Sobek. "There is love—a fire set aglow in your heart, warming the core of your soul, blanketing you in serene, utter peace. Allowing your unrestrained mind to drift to places it could not before—places where every breath infuses you with purpose and each glint of dancing candlelight reminds you that you are fragile and finite. The revelation sends a tremor through your heart that makes your pulse skip a beat. And though you are exposed and raw, you are not afraid, because it makes you feel whole and gives reason to life."

The room went completely silent, and Ra did not respond to my words.

Another glint of magic fluttered over my skin.

"But with love and affection, come loss and grief," I continued, "and if it is your belief that being turned mortal should be a punishment, then you have never held a dead child in your arms, for it is far worse a feeling than this."

Ra's skin began to fade, and his golden headdress lost much of its sparkle, turning dull with tarnish. My hands trembled with wild energy. A rush of magic rippled through my veins and everything became a little brighter and a little more colorful as my vision changed.

"You call yourselves gods," I said. "The all-knowing few who govern the earth as you believe it should be governed, and yet, you know nothing of what it is to *actually live*. All because of an archaic oath which claims to protect us from favoritism by banning us from empathy. Ra claims I am young and inexperienced and, yet, he is as naïve as a child, and he forces that ignorance upon you all."

"Silence! I will not allow you to spew blasphemous things in my court!" Ra roared and towered over me, a magical aura emanating from his hands. "He spits lies in an effort to confuse and sway you."

"I speak only truth," I replied, a shot of brilliant light igniting my eyes, too.

"He *does* speak truth," a soft, feminine voice announced.

My mother entered the courtyard, her grand, iridescent wings shimmering with vibrant colors again.

Ra looked past me, at her. "You have no say in this matter."

As Osiris' wife and queen, Isis was one of the most revered and respected goddesses in the kingdom; her opinion *did* matter.

"He is my son, and I will speak for him," she replied. "I have witnessed these things. Because I neglected my duties and allowed a girl to perish in my own temple in the mortal realm, the death of an innocent child haunts me.

"But the blame does not fall upon me, alone. The child wandered the night because she was in search of the priestess who had disappeared while caring for my son's near-fatal wound. Horus was vulnerable and weak without his magic, and Set had attempted to murder him by assuming the form of one of Wadjet's children. With Horus suspended in the shadow of death, Set encroached upon my husband's throne. These events caused a series of grave consequences to follow, and you, Lord Ra, stood idly by, turning a blind eye to them all. This makes you equally accountable and guilty of breaking the Oath."

"The child was expendable," Ra replied, "but Horus did not have permission to seduce my priestess and make her his own."

"A god should consider no child expendable," Isis pointed out. "As for your priestess, it was not until *after* you bestowed mortality upon my son that she accepted him as her husband and began considering a life outside your temple. She may have loved Horus before he bled mortal blood, but Horus did not know what it was to love her until *you* gifted him that pleasure." Isis lifted her chin and stood straighter. "Do not threaten me, my son, or his wife."

Ra glared at her, but then switched targets and looked at me again. "You stole that *alleged* wife from my temple. You stole my power."

"So you admit it, then?" I replied. "You admit that the mortals are responsible for what we are?"

Ra froze up and his eyes grew wide and dark.

"You have ruled over them for centuries," I said. "Day after day, year after year, you watch them die. What have you learned from their sacrifices? That they are mere sheep? You know nothing about those who worship us and give up their lives in our names."

I raised my free hand, placed it on my chest, and looked out at the crowd. "The amulet Ra gave me was destroyed by Set at my trial. To restore some of my power, and to help them find Osiris' missing heart, Bastet, Wadjet, and Anubis forged a similar stone with fragments of their magic encased inside. I wear it as a symbol of those who have stood by me, but the piece is now powerless—dull and empty. Yet, my skin glows and there is new life in me since I have arrived back. This magic exists only because you believe my words, and because there are humans on Earth who have faith in the Sky God, Horus."

Ra's rage sparked again and he lifted his arms and cut the air with his hands, orchestrating a spell with great fervor.

But no light came to his fingertips. And no fire was stoked in his eyes. He continued to try, grunting and hissing as he swirled his hands about in a second futile attempt to conjure what was likely an attack.

I opened my hands and gazed down at my fingertips, which were glowing with an aura of fair white light.

Ra panted angrily and thrashed his arms about in disbelief. "This cannot be!" he yelped, his strength visibly dwindling as the details of his face and jewelry lost saturation and depth.

"The throne of the underworld is Horus' by descent, but the Palace of the Gods could be his by decision of his peers," Isis said, addressing the other gods.

I was shaking now, unsure if I wanted what the other gods might be willing to give me, but I was not about to decline it. I needed to be there for Zahra, as I had promised. And having Ra's powers would help me do that. But I did not wish to forgo the emotions I had acquired as a human, either.

"Let me lead you, as both mortal and immortal," I suggested, looking past Ra, at the other gods. I could not stop thinking about Zahra. I wanted her back, and I would not sacrifice her for this kingdom, but I also knew that the court had already begun to choose me; I could feel it. "Allow me to rule as a human god—immortal by choice—who is able to experience and share with you what it is to feel, so that I may understand our followers and serve them better, in exchange for their trust in us."

Ra approached me and reached for my necklace. But when he came forward, his hand passed through my chest, and a look of dread creased his face. "How is this possible!?" he asked, trying to mask the panic in his voice.

Knowing it was my chance to strike, I turned to the

crowd and spoke, "Make your choice."

A horrendous roar rumbled through the floor; Ra hunched over and charged me like a raging bull. The cauldron in the center of the room flared, and he crashed into me with the force of a subtle breeze, fading upon impact.

Both hands tingled with a rush of golden magic and fire burned through my veins. My tattoo shimmered and the vibrancy of my skin intensified.

The place fell eerily quiet and I looked out at the sea of beastly faces bowing toward me.

Ra had vanished...

The gods lifted their heads, and I was taken aback by how quickly they began filing out of the courtyard, returning to their duties with no arguments to be had.

"W-what happens now?" I asked, turning toward Isis.

"Your father will be proud," she replied, putting her hand on my shoulder. "They have chosen you to take Ra's place, and their renewed faith has restored your immortality and magic."

I did not quite understand everything that had happened, yet. "I will do my best," I said. "Thank you for standing with me here. I do not wish to abandon you so quickly, but I would like to check on Zahra."

"I understand." She smiled and then bowed her head.

My fingers flexed on the Staff of Justice and I envisioned myself in the Temple of Ra. The ground disappeared from beneath my feet and a gust of wind swept me up, carrying me through the sky without the need for wings. I flew through the darkness, toward the village, and then down toward the temple entryway.

I landed on the sand and stone pathway, between the statues of Ra that sat guarding it on each side. With a flick of my fingers, I changed their forms to represent my own, slimming the over-exaggerated features into those which were more natural, and *human*.

I extinguished the lamps outside the temple and then walked inside. The other wives were asleep, and I was quiet on my feet as I made my way back toward Zahra's ceremonial chamber. My hand lifted toward the door and I tapped the carved sun with my knuckles.

"Zahra?" I whispered.

I heard nothing, so I willed the lock to open and it clicked. The doors began to part and I peeked inside. Zahra sat on the edge of her bed with her face in her hands, sobbing.

"Zahra?" I spoke quietly, so as to not startle her.

Her face rose and she gasped. "Horus!?" She came to her feet and wiped her reddened cheeks with both hands, swiping away tears. "You are alive!" She rushed toward me and I laid the staff on the floor at my feet so that I could take her into my arms and embrace her tightly.

"I could not sleep knowing that you fought great battles in the night," she said, nuzzling against my chest and squeezing me in closer. "I feared for your life, but I had faith in you and I hoped, with all my heart, that you would return to me."

"And you were right to do so," I said, kissing her. "I had fully intended to come back to you."

Her warm skin beneath my fingertips was wonderful. I wanted to forget everything that had happened and steal her away from this place, as I had promised to, but...

"I must tell you something." I released her and cupped her cheek with my hand.

"Your eyes!?" She noticed the differing colors.

"Wadjet gave me one of hers, because... Set tore one from me. But I see as well as I had before. I hope you will accept me with it."

"Of course, my love. It does not change who you are. Now what is it you must tell me?"

I swallowed hard. "Ra is no more, and the gods have chosen me to take his place."

Her eyes opened wide. "*You* have become... King of the Gods?"

"It would seem so, but I asked to retain my physical body, so that I might rule as a human and a god, and still know what it is to be alive. I would have given all my magic to be with you, but I did not have to."

Sadness washed over Zahra's face and she sighed and looked away from me. "Does this mean that *I* will die a mortal death, and that you will live on without me?"

"I-I do not know," I replied, trying to resist the infectious sorrow. "I—"

A colorful beam of light manifested in the room and I pulled Zahra close to shield her from it.

The light twirled, sparkled, and then came together into a familiar form.

"Mother?" My grasp on Zahra loosened and she immediately fell to her knees and bowed.

"You do not need to bow to me," Isis spoke, approaching Zahra and bending down to offer her a hand. "My daughter-in-law shall not bow to me."

Zahra lifted her face and then her hand to take my mother's. She was trembling, but smiling.

"Can you answer that question, Mother?" I asked. "What of her life span?" I reached for Zahra's hand. "Will she die a mortal?"

Isis frowned. "I am afraid we cannot create new gods," she replied. "We can only give and take from the energy that surrounds us."

My heart sank and Zahra squeezed my hand.

I would give up my position if it meant—

"You were destined to be great, my son." Isis brushed her fingertips across my cheek and smiled; the confident and assuring look made my heart feel a little lighter. "Do not worry, Horus. I wish to revive and strengthen my duties as the guardian of mothers and children, and I wish to start by protecting your wife and child."

"C-child?"

Zahra and I glanced at each other and then back at Isis.

A wide grin stretched across her face and she nodded, lifting her fingers toward us to reveal a subtle golden aura surrounding Zahra.

"Your wife is with child; it will not be long before you hold a babe of your own flesh and blood in your arms."

A child!? But... would the child be human, god, or... both?

I let out an anxious laugh.

It did not matter, for I would love them all the same.

My mouth hung open and my heart fluttered with excitement.

Then a shadow of doubt and fear reared its head and I

shuddered, contemplating how exactly Zahra could stay with me if she were to remain mortal.

"I can grant her a lifeforce similar to what the other gods have given you," my mother continued, "and it will suspend her mortality indefinitely. That is... *if* you, as our new king, will it of me."

"Yes," I replied without pause. "With everything I have ever been and will ever be." A feverish joy roiled in my chest, making me tremble with happiness and spill tears that were not from sadness.

The glow surrounding my wife began to strengthen and the warmth of her hand in mine tingled like tiny sparks of fire against my skin.

"I will return to the palace," Isis added, "and request that the other gods prepare a place for you both."

"I... think I wish to stay here a little longer," I replied, pulling Zahra in close to my side.

"Of course." My mother bowed her head. "But you must be back before dawn, if you are to keep our sun from falling prey to the serpent, Apep."

"I understand." My gaze fell upon the Staff of Justice, which I had set down by the entryway. "It is my hope that I will vanquish the beast, for good."

Isis disappeared in a flash of rainbow light.

I looked back down at Zahra and smiled. "I have and will always keep my promise to you," I said, finding comfort in her earthy brown eyes.

I wanted to experience mortal emotion for eternity, so that I could share the hauntingly beautiful feeling of human sentiment. Pain. Joy. Love. And I wished to rule with a brave and kind wife by my side, to remind me always of those strange and wondrous things.

I had earned the head priestess of Ra's devotion, precisely as I had hoped many moons ago.

Except now, I had become her sun, and she had become mine...

Thank you for reading!

If you enjoyed this story, please support the author in her writing journey by posting a review on Amazon or social media. Share your thoughts with friends, other readers, and book clubs.

More from P. Anastasia:

Fates Aflame & Fates Awoken

Adventure that will lift your spirits and romance to warm your heart

Magical journeys await you in this clean epic sci-fi fantasy. With newfound powers at hand and a dragon by her side, Lt. Hawksford, star student of a prestigious military academy, must face trial by fire.

Dark Diary

A historical love story with supernatural undertones

When a 17th-century vampire meets a modern tattoo artist tormented by visions of her own death, their dark pasts unite them. More human than vampire, this unique, sophisticated romance details the accounts of two old souls burdened by tragedy.

Fluorescence: The Complete Tetralogy

An infectious saga read across the world

Alice was a normal teenager until a dying race of aliens chose her to preserve their bioluminescent DNA. Fluorescence evolves from quiet beginnings into a gripping tale exploring the real-life dangers faced while harboring a volatile secret.

The series includes:

Book 1: Fire Starter
Book 2: Contagious
Book 3: Fallout
Book 4: Lost Souls

P. Anastasia's fresh take on storytelling resonates with darkness, charm, and passion—the embodiment of her unique writing style. With origins tracing back to the late eighties, the creative light that became Exile of the Sky God was drawn from P.'s fascination with archeology, ancient Egyptian mythology, and all things magical.

Ensnared by the craft in childhood, she attempted her first book at age eleven. While working toward her college degree, she wrote news and editorial columns for two campus newspapers. After graduating with a degree in communications and spending a year studying abroad in Kofu, Japan, she followed her heart to her publishing aspirations. She currently resides in the beautiful, green state of Kentucky with her husband and her ever-inspiring fur-babies. On the side, she serves as a professional voice talent for radio, television, and audio books.

P. Anastasia is the author of eight novels: the *Fluorescence* series, *Fates Aflame,* and the historical-paranormal romance, *Dark Diary*.

www.ingramcontent.com/pod-product-compliance
Lightning Source LLC
Chambersburg PA
CBHW020525310726
48979CB00014B/2213/J

* 9 7 8 0 9 9 7 4 4 8 5 7 3 *